JEAN .

The
LEGEND

Red Deer Press

Published in Canada by Red Deer Press,
195 Allstate Parkway, Markham, ON L3R 4T8

Published in the United States by Red Deer Press,
311 Washington Street, Brighton, MA 02135

Red Deer Press acknowledges with thanks the Canada Council for the Arts and the Ontario Arts Council for
their support of our publishing program. We acknowledge the financial support of the
Government of Canada through the Canada Book Fund (CBF) for our publishing activities.

Edited for the Press by Peter Carver
Text and cover design by Tanya Montini
Proudly printed in Canada by Avant Imaging & Integrated Media

Library and Archives Canada Cataloguing in Publication
Title: The legend / Jean Mills.
Names: Mills, Jean, 1955- author.
Identifiers: Canadiana 20210209747 | ISBN 9780889956407 (softcover)
Subjects: LCGFT: Novels.
Classification: LCC PS8576.I5654 L44 2021 | DDC jC813/.54—dc23

Publisher Cataloging-in-Publication Data (U.S.)
Names: Mills, Jean, 1955-, author.
Title: The Legend / Jean Mills.
Description: Markham, Ontario : Red Deer Press, 2021. | Summary: "Griffin
Tardiff, 16, sidelined from hockey because of a serious injury, starts Grade 11
in a new school an hour away from his home town of Ottawa. He chooses, as
his community service, a spot at the local radio station. Then he gets involved
in the lives of a family in his new neighborhood which opens his eyes to other
intriguing possibilities" -- Provided by publisher.
Identifiers: ISBN 978-0-88995-640-7 (paperback)
Subjects: LCSH: Hockey players -- Juvenile fiction. | Emotional maturity
-- Juvenile fiction. | Intergenerational relations -- Juvenile fiction. | BISAC:
YOUNG ADULT FICTION / Coming of Age.
Classification: LCC PZ7.M555Le | DDC 813.6 – dc23

Red Deer Press
www.reddeerpress.com

For Peter Carver,
editor extraordinaire

*To write is human,
to edit is divine.*
– Stephen King

NIGHT

The pain wakes me up again.

Six months and the pain still wakes me up. The doctor said you never can tell with a fractured humerus.

"It's quite high up, but it could have been worse, Griffin. Could have been a seriously messed-up shoulder. We just have to let the bone heal and work on getting that range of motion back with physio, resistance bands. Cautious progression of weight-bearing exercise. Can't predict the length of time it will take to be pain free, though."

Blah blah, doctor talk.

"When can I play hockey again?"

He shrugged. "You will play hockey again, Griff, but you need to take this slowly. To do it right."

So, I'm doing it right and the pain still wakes me up at night.

Or maybe it's not the pain. Maybe it's the thought of tomorrow.

First day of Grade 11 at a new school, here in this borrowed house in the town of Glenavon, down the highway from Ottawa. Our home for a year while Dad does his thing, setting up a new program for his college at a bunch of satellite campuses around the southern part of the region. Yeah, he's got a lot of driving ahead of him, even with this one-year move.

I lie on my back in this unfamiliar room and stare at the ceiling. Whoever lived here before stuck star stickers up there and, every now and then, one catches the light from the streetlight outside as the breeze blows the curtains around. I'll have to ask Mom if we can install blinds. I need my room to be dark. It helps.

Helps with the pain. Helps me relax. Helps keep out the image of that last crushing play, my last moment in our playoff game, and the boards rushing up to meet me, and the crack of the bone as it was demolished.

I reach over for my earbuds and phone, find my "Middle of the Night Chill" playlist and roll over onto my good right arm.

Close my eyes and imagine skating down the Rideau Canal in February. Drift off.

A half-hour later, the pain wakes me up again.

NEW KID

Two texts buzz their arrival while Mom and I are sitting outside the principal's office next morning. We look at each other.

"Do you think I can take my phone out? Will they expel me and send me back to Ottawa?"

She gives me the Mom Look—*Nice try, kid*—but she follows that up with her nod-shrug thing, which means it's up to me.

"You're not officially a student here yet, so ..."

"True."

Phone out.

Miss you already. Good luck today xo

Blair, my is-she-or-isn't-she girlfriend. It's complicated, mostly complicated by Blair, who is one minute hanging off me as if I'm the center of her universe, and the next minute is laughing it up with Jake or Evan or one of the other guys on the team. I find this confusing. Sending out mixed signals seems to be her standard setting. This text is promising, but a whole school year away from her? I don't know.

Thanks. Miss you too

I draw the line at emojis and xo's though, and I'm pretty sure she knows that by now.

Beside me on these uncomfortable chairs, Mom shifts a little and glances at her phone. She's all about action, my mother. She teaches at the same college as Dad, and this year, she'll teach a couple of courses at the local campus but spend most of her time designing a new course to be added to the Office Administration program back in Ottawa. One school year here in Glenavon, that's the plan. She says she's looking forward to a year with a lighter workload, time to "recharge," but I don't know. I think she's already antsy.

"The principal must be having fun with somebody," she whispers to me, keeping her eyes on the closed office door beyond the reception counter. *Mrs. Margaret McRae.*

Great. Already running late on my first day of school. Which is actually the second day of school at Glenavon Collegiate Institute. Moving complications and some of Dad's college administration stuff delayed everything, so here I am, making the one-day-late big entrance.

I glance down at the other text. Jake. My best friend since forever. My centerman. My teammate. The one who skated over, knelt beside me as I was writhing out on the ice, and yelled for the trainer to come quick, and the doctor. Who wouldn't get out of the way when they brought out the backboard and got yelled at by the ref. Who skated all the way to the exit with us as they wheeled me off the ice. I might have been crying in pain, but Jake was there. "You've got this, bud," I remember him saying.

School sucks

I'm just ready to text him back, when Mom jabs me with her elbow and leans into my ear.

"Showtime."

Phone away just in time. Mrs. Margaret McRae's door has opened and she's walking toward us. She's not alone, though. This morning's Meeting No. 1 is walking ahead of her—a girl with short black hair tossed around by a handful of product. Eyes focused on the floor like she's following a line. She's wearing black—a tunic thing and leggings. Boots. Not Goth, exactly—not enough makeup—but definitely making some sort of artsy statement. She also has a pair of really good headphones looped around her neck, attached to the high-performance phone in her hand. So, phones in the principal's office are okay, I guess?

"Have a good first day back, Rose," says Mrs. McRae. "And before you head to class, say hello to Griffin. He's new at GCI this year and he'll be in your homeroom."

There is nothing worse than adults doing the "Hey kids, be

friends" thing, but this girl Rose and I do our duty, nod at each other, briefly make eye contact.

"Hi," she says and keeps walking.

"Hi," I say and, as she slips by us toward the door, I realize I know this girl.

No, I don't know her, but I saw her. Last night, on our street. As I stood in my new room, looking out at my view for the next ten months, she walked by—I mean, who could miss that all-black fashion statement?—with a kid, a boy. A young boy. They both had their heads down as they walked, and she had an arm draped around his shoulders. I couldn't hear what they said, but the kid was chattering away, and she was answering with squeezes of her arm, leaning down to answer him. Big sister, little brother is my guess.

"So, Griffin, hi. And Mrs. Tardiff, hello." The handshaking, smiling, and nodding commences. "Welcome to Glenavon," says Mrs. McRae. "Come along in and we'll get this day started as quickly as possible. Sorry for the wait."

"No problem at all," says Mom, all gracious and light, and not letting on that a minute ago, she was glancing at her phone and telling me it was okay to pull out mine and text at school. "We're so happy to be here."

The meeting is mostly about signing papers (Mom) and learning the rules (me). For instance, no cell phones during class, but okay between classes and in the lunchroom, etc. etc., so I (and Rose) apparently haven't broken any rules yet.

"And I see you missed some school with an injury last year, Griffin. But you were able to make up courses online over the summer—and you're up-to-date on your prerequisites for Grade 11. Good." Mrs. McRae is looking at her computer screen and typing a little, probably tapped into that secret file-keeping world that belongs to school administrators. I picture my principal back in Ottawa, Mr. Pike, eyes also on his screen in his office at this very moment. Maybe they're messaging each other.

Pike: Good student, nice kid, never in trouble, but bad luck on the hockey team last year.

McRae: If you say so. Caught him texting in the office on his first day here.

"And we have your medical form, too, with the instructions about your injury and gym class restrictions. Great—everything seems to be in order," Mrs. McRae says, turning back to us and smiling. "Shall we head off to your homeroom, Griffin? Get this school year started?"

"Sure, thanks."

Sure. Let's get this one-year exile, away from our familiar house, away from Jake and Blair, away from hockey—sure, let's get this school year started so it can end, and everything can go back to normal.

11

COMMUNITY SERVICE

"Sorry, guys, but there are only a few options left," says Mr. Dunbar, the 11B homeroom teacher. "Everyone else picked theirs yesterday."

I can hear the smirks—yes, it's possible to hear smirks—of the rest of the class as Rose and I glance at our handouts for the Community Service positions. She's sitting on the other side of the room near the front, but I managed to land a desk near the back. I can see her up there, head bent over the paper.

I read it over quickly, because it feels like a race to pick something halfway decent, something I can actually stand, for this required community service that everyone at this school has to do in Grade 11.

"We do it this way to keep students' schedules free for Grade 12 and all that university application prep you're going to be doing," Mr. Dunbar explained to me as he handed me the list.

Rose just took the paper and started scanning, but apparently he feels I needed some explanation.

So now I'm scanning and it's not looking good. Everything is crossed off except for three options.

Assist with the entertainment program at Avonlea Seniors Lodge. This important job involves interacting with seniors in our long-term care residence to provide friendly companionship, including games, conversation, and possible special projects. CPR required. For students interested in nursing, teaching, recreation.

Work in the office of the Glenavon cemetery. Indulge your love of genealogy and support community history by helping with the updating and reorganization of local files and records. Typing and familiarity with Excel are required. For students who are interested in history, library science, business administration.

Assist with on-air content at community radio station, The Legend 99.1. May include any of the following: writing copy for website and on-air advertising; supplying information for on-air news and/or sports coverage. Strong communication and media/technical skills required. For students interested in media studies or journalism.

I read them quickly. Obviously, of the three, there's only one real choice.

A radio station. Broadcasting. My dream job. And just as I look up, just as I'm about to raise my hand ...

"Rose? You've decided?" says Mr. Dunbar.

"But, sir ..." One of the guys near the front is leaning over, looking at Rose's sheet as she sits there with her hand up. "That Legend 99.1 posting wasn't there yesterday."

He's got a bit of a whine going on and I look at him more closely. A big guy, I'm guessing a jock.

"True, Bradley. Mr. Martin didn't know we were picking yesterday and called this morning with this opportunity for us."

Rose makes a sound, something between a snort and a laugh, and Mr. Dunbar nods at her. "Yes, Rose? What have you decided?"

My hand is up but I'm too late. Mr. Dunbar hasn't noticed me yet, and I feel my dream going up in smoke. Because, of course, I can tell by looking at her and her high-tech headphones that Rose is not a fun-at-the-cemetery or hanging-out-with-the-seniors kind of girl.

"I'll take Avonlea," she says.

"Great. Thanks," says Mr. Dunbar, making a note on his computer.

It takes me a moment to process the idea that Rose is, in fact, a hanging-out-with-the-seniors kind of girl, despite the tech gear.

And another moment to realize that Mr. Dunbar has turned to me and called my name. Twice. And everyone is starting to stare.

"I'll take the radio station," I say, and suddenly the school year seems full of possibilities.

"Great ... that's done. We'll go into detail later about the community service requirements, reports and everything, but not today." He makes another note on the computer and then picks up a paper and turns back to the class. "Now, gang, last item of business before everyone heads off to your first class of the day," and he launches into something about the upcoming Curriculum Night.

I glance across the room at Rose and she's looking at me, an expression on her face that I can't decipher. Just a flash of eye contact, and then she turns back to the front.

LUNCHROOM

"Hey, Griffin ... over here," says someone at a table to my left, as I wander into the cafeteria and look around for somewhere to sit and hide. The morning has been a bit overwhelming.

I turn and see Bradley the jock—Brad to anyone who's not a teacher—sitting there with a few other guys and giving me the nod.

"Come on, new boy, join the team here," he says.

They do look like a team, actually. The height, the pumped-up arms, the shoulders-back posture—I'd put my money on this being a gathering of the school's senior hockey team.

"Thanks." I take the empty seat beside a tall blond guy who looks like he just stepped off the plane from Sweden and (my guess) plays defense. We nod at each other.

"Hi, I'm Mike," he says. Smiles.

"Griffin." I nod at him.

"So, this is the guy who landed the best community service

job on the planet," Brad leans forward to tell the other guys, all of whom are in various stages of lunch consumption. "At The Legend 99.1." He uses what I guess he thinks is a radio voice, but it just sounds kind of stupid. That doesn't matter to the other guys, though. They all look at me with expressions of envy.

"Oh, man, you're so lucky," says a beefy guy who has to be a goalie. (I'm keeping track of my predictions now.) He was in my math class earlier today and I'm pretty sure his name is Kyle Murphy.

"No kidding," says Brad. "Where was this job yesterday when the rest of us had to pick? Guy must have been afraid one of us would take it."

They all laugh at that. Bad boys, obviously. Reputations to build and live up to. I have my egg sandwich out now and am keeping my eye on them as this conversation progresses. Eventually, someone might get around to including me but, for now, I know the drill. They're just establishing their perimeter with The New Guy.

"I would have taken it like that," says Kyle, snapping his fingers.

"You'd suck at radio, Murph. You can't even read out loud in class," says Shane, also from math class, who wears a Senators T-shirt that shows off his weight-room-honed pecs and biceps.

The guys all laugh but Murph doesn't seem to mind.

"C'mon. That was Shakespeare," he says. Which tells me everything I need to know about Murph.

"So, Griff, you're going to be the radio guy. Do you know anything about sports? 'Cause if Guy Martin is your supervisor, there will be a ton of sports stuff going on," says Brad. (I'm sure he's a center. Maybe the captain. Still gathering intel.)

It's actually a fair question because, looking at me, you'd never know I'm all about hockey. You might not believe that I won the Rookie of the Year award for our school in Grade 9. That I won the scoring title for our entire high school league in Grade 10, even with the injury. Or that I was an All-Star both years (although that might have been a pity award last season—I can't be sure).

Looking at me sitting there, downing my egg sandwich, they're probably thinking I'm too small, but what they can't see is that I'm fast, maybe the fastest skater on any team I've ever been part of. I can find the spaces and get there first. I have good hands (say all my coaches) and a gift for anticipation.

I just didn't anticipate that defenseman from Owen Sound taking me into the boards at the provincial high school playoffs, breaking my arm just below the shoulder, and ruining my life for the next six months.

"You a runner?" asks Mike, and I like him for it because it's a fair question. I am actually built a lot like a runner.

"No. Hockey."

Brad leans forward. "Really?" And I know he wants to add: *A little guy like you?*—but he doesn't. Maybe he's not a jerk after all. "What position?"

"Center."

The guys all laugh and look at Brad. "Competition for you, Scotty." Bradley Scott, right.

And Brad's looking at me now, too, considering me. "You trying out for the team?" He waves around the table at the six other guys sitting there. "'Cause if you are, meet the team."

They all look at me, waiting. I put down my sandwich and look back. Then at Brad.

"No tryouts. No hockey for me for a while. I broke my arm pretty badly at the end of the season, and my doctor won't let me go back on the ice yet."

I don't say anything about the ongoing pain, or the hours of reps with resistance bands, with weights. The ice packs. The x-rays. The number of times I've heard, "Not yet, Griffin," and, "Yes, it's improving, but no contact sports yet." And the worst: "No hockey."

"Sucks, man," says Mike. "Must have been a bad break if you're out for so long."

"It was." I don't want to get into it. Time to change the subject. "But hey, maybe I'll get to report on the school team or something. For this job at the radio station, I mean."

"Yeah, maybe." Brad shrugs, then leans forward. "But a lot of The Legend's coverage goes to the Moose."

He and a couple of the other guys start up with some deep, bleacher-friendly chant involving the repetition of the word "moose," accompanied by foot stomping. People at tables nearby pick it up and join in, and it all ends with a huge roar and a bunch of wild applause from most of the room.

"You know the Moose is our local Junior A team, right?" Mike explains this to me while everyone settles back down. Brad actually has to climb down off his chair, under the boss gaze of a male teacher over near the door. It's all friendly and cool, though. Clearly Brad is considered harmless.

The Prescott Moose, of course. The league extends throughout the eastern part of the province, a sort of farm league for the OHL. I didn't realize Glenavon was the home base of the Moose.

"Right ... cool. They did well last season, didn't they?"

"Lost in the finals," Mike says. "It was brutal."

"Anyway," Brad interrupts, leaning in so he can get everyone's attention down the table, "we now have an insider at The Legend, so maybe it's our turn for some love from Guy Martin during the season, right? Right?" And they all look at me.

"I'll see what I can do." No promises.

"Maybe you'll be the next Josh Drouin," says Murph. "He's 'The Legend' from The Legend. You know he started out here, too, eh?"

Now, that is interesting. Josh Drouin, the youngest guy on the hockey broadcasts, especially Ottawa-based stuff. The guy who does rinkside interviews during NHL games, catches the players between the bench and dressing room for a few quick questions during intermission. Everybody who watches hockey knows Josh Drouin.

"Guy Martin taught him everything he knows," says Brad. "Maybe you're next, bud. The next Legend."

Not quite sure how to respond to that, but it doesn't matter, because I've finished my sandwich, and a glance at my phone reminds me that we only have ten minutes before next class. English. And I promised Mom I'd check in at lunch. Which is a nugget I don't intend to share with The Team.

"Yeah, maybe," I say, packing up my lunch and stuffing the containers back into my pack. "Hey, thanks for this, guys. I've got to go—figure out what I'm doing next class. Go to my locker and everything. See you all later."

"See you around," says Mike and he nods at me, as if he knows everything I've been thinking about Brad and his boss-man attitude, about Murph the goalie, about Shane and his pecs. We grin at each other, and I figure I've found my first friend at Glenavon.

BALL HOCKEY

Forehand, backhand, forehand, dangle (and let's just say it's hard to dangle with a tennis ball), wrist shot ...

Ouch. *Shit!*

Something about the angle of my arm, I don't know. Dad would say it's physics. Dr. Fitzpatrick would say if it hurts, I should stop doing it. Mom just gave me a look when I told her I was going to set up the net on the driveway and see if, just see if ...

I don't look up to see if she's watching me from the living room window, but I bet she is.

Retrieve the ball from the net (because, of course, I hit the net, painful broken arm recovery or not) and stickhandle it back down the driveway. Maybe if I get a bit closer, shorten up with my left hand.

Forehand, backhand, forehand, no dangle. Wrist shot.

Ouch.

"Shit!" More than just a thought this time.

"Hey!"

I whip around and there's a little kid standing at the end of the driveway, watching me with a huge smile on his face. And, yes, he just heard me swear, which is probably not cool.

I glance at the living room window. No Mom. Good.

"Hey," I say back to him.

I don't ask why he's standing at the end of my driveway, watching me take shots. I'm still trying to get over the pain that just shot up and down my arm.

He's not selling anything that I can see. No box of chocolate bars or clipboard with sign-up sheet for Christmas poinsettias or cookie dough. (Yes, I know all about sports team fundraising drives, and I've done every one of them. More than once.)

"You're Griffin Tardiff," he says, still smiling away as if this is his best day ever. His hands are pulling at his Ottawa Senators T-shirt, as if he's nervous. Or really excited.

But this is weird. Why does this kid know my name?

"Yeah, I'm Griffin," I say. "And—you're ...?"

"I'm Noah. Noah Courville. Rosie's my sister. You know, Rosie Courville from school. Rosie, you know? Rosie?"

He's a funny little kid, and now I recognize him. Last night, walking past the house with Rose, the two of them deep in conversation, her arm around his shoulders. I don't know how he knows my name, though.

"Hi, Noah. And, yeah … Rose … Rosie." I pause, thinking he might say something else to explain, but he just stands there smiling at me. Kid's a bit weird. But then, I thought his sister was a bit weird, too. "So, what's up?"

"I like hockey," he says, huge smile. "No, I *love* hockey."

I stickhandle a little closer. Kid obviously wants to talk and … hey, I'm okay with little kids who want to talk hockey, especially kids wearing Sens gear.

"Do you play?"

"Nah. My mom won't let me because it's too expensive."

Okay, I wasn't expecting that. "That's too bad. When you love it so much."

"Yeah, I love watching it, though." His eyes are on my stick as I fiddle with the tennis ball, forehand, backhand, forehand, backhand.

He's a funny kid but, man, I hate the "it's too expensive" part because, unfortunately, it's true.

"I've got another stick in the garage," I say. Actually, I've got a dozen sticks in the garage. "D'you want to take some shots with me?"

It's Christmas for Noah. The look on his face makes me laugh.

"C'mon, bud."

So we take shots. He's actually not bad, especially considering that my stick is too long for him. But he adapts and shows some pretty good stuff once he gets rolling. He laughs every time he hits the net.

"Not bad," I say. "Okay, I'll pass to you and you put it in."

"Just like ..." He names an NHL left-winger everybody knows, who loves to stand on the edge of the crease and deflect roofers into the net. The kid does know his hockey.

"Yeah, just like him."

I'm impressed. The kid has good hands, and he tucks three straight passes into the net.

We're high-fiving when she calls him.

"Hey, Noah. Time for supper."

It's Rose ... Rosie. In our hat-trick excitement, we didn't see her there at the end of the driveway. She's still wearing her school uniform of leggings and Docs and a black tunic thing, denim jacket. No headphones, though.

"Aw, Rosie ... do I have to?"

"Yup. Mom's leaving for work soon and you need to eat. So come on. Say thanks."

She looks at me then. No smile, just a nod of acknowledgment. Like I'm a random stranger who's been looking after her little brother.

"Okay." Noah looks at me then, holding out the stick. "I gotta go, Griffin. Thanks. Can I come back sometime? Come back and take shots?"

"Sure. Anytime you see me out here," I say. "Come on over." Then, I don't know why, but this just happens. "Why don't you keep the stick, bud. And here's the tennis ball. Maybe you can practice on your own driveway."

"Can I?" His face is blank with shock and then he starts to smile. "Can I? Keep it?"

"Sure. I've got lots of sticks." Probably not the nicest thing to say to a kid who has just told me his family can't afford to let him play hockey, but I want him—want her, actually—to know that it's not a big deal.

"Rosie! Look!"

"You don't need to do that," she says, not looking at me. Looking at Noah and his stick.

"I know. I want to." I'm willing her to look at me, but she doesn't. These two kids are both a bit strange, if you ask me. "He's good. And he had fun."

Noah is beside her now, starting down the sidewalk to wherever their house is. Somewhere down the block, I guess. He holds the stick in one hand, the tennis ball in the other, as if he's that guy at the opening of parliament with the ceremonial orb and scepter.

"Well, thank you."

"You're welcome," I say, but she's already turned away and is walking down the sidewalk with her little brother, listening to him chattering about taking shots with Griffin, carrying his stick and ball as if they're treasures.

I still haven't figured out how he knew my name, though. Unless she told him.

THE LEGEND

"That was nice," says Mom, when I come into the kitchen from the mud room after putting the net away in the garage.

I knew she'd been watching. Probably heard me swear, too, even though I didn't see her standing at the window.

I just shrug. "I have lots of sticks."

"Yes, you do." She turns back to the counter and her cheese shredder. Mom's Famous Baked Macaroni for supper tonight, obviously. "But it was still nice of you."

I steal a clump of grated cheese and she pretends to be mad. We've been doing this act since ... I don't know ... maybe forever? Since I had to drag the little stepstool over so I could see over the counter.

On the table by the mud-room door, where we drop keys and phones and mail, my phone gives its email ding. I touch the screen with my uncheesed hand and open my mail.

From someone named Elise Rogers. No idea who that is.

Subject: Welcome to The Legend 99.1!

Normally I'd wash my hands before handling my phone, but this can't wait. Keeping the cheesy hand away, I navigate to the full message.

Hi Griffin,

I'm the Station Manager at The Legend 99.1. Mr. Dunbar, your homeroom teacher at the high school, let me know that you've agreed to be our student intern to meet your community service requirement this term, and we're delighted.

The Legend 99.1 has been serving Glenavon and the surrounding region for almost thirty years, and we're committed to involving the community in our programming. Many of our broadcasters and technicians are volunteers, but we do have a small professional staff to coordinate, administer, and deliver the programming of this award-winning community radio station. Welcome aboard!

Could you please drop by the station tomorrow or Friday afternoon after school so we can meet? I'd like to discuss your role here, your and our expectations, etc. I'm sure you have questions as well. Let me know which day works best for you and I'll make sure I'm available.

Mr. Dunbar mentioned that you have a sports background,

so perhaps you would be interested in doing some of your duties alongside our longtime Sports Director, Guy Martin. It was Guy who suggested partnering with the high school to offer this opportunity to interested students.

Looking forward to meeting you, Griffin. Again, welcome aboard!

Best,

Elise

_____

Elise Rogers
Station Manager
The Legend 99.1

I reply right away, of course.

Hi Elise,

Thanks for getting in touch so quickly. I could drop by the station on Thursday (tomorrow) after school at about 3:45 PM. Does that work for you?

I'm really looking forward to talking to you about this opportunity. I do have a sports background (mostly hockey), so working with your Sports Director would be great.

Thanks again for this opportunity. Hope to see you tomorrow.

Griffin Tardiff

I have to go find the screen cleaner now because I've cheesed all over my phone, but who cares. This is the best thing that's happened since my parents told me they were uprooting me from Ottawa and forcing me into exile down here for a year.

If I can't play hockey this year, okay. Maybe I can report on it. Maybe I can be the next Josh Drouin. The Legend.

TRYOUT

"Let's see what you've got," says Guy Martin, the sports guy at The Legend 99.1.

We're in his office. Office? Too generous a word, maybe. It's about the size of a clothes closet. Cluttered desk. Him on one side, me on the other. He has a laptop open, and he turns it so we can both see the screen.

It's a YouTube video of highlights from a game during last season. The game where Nathan McCormick scored a hat trick for the Flames and demolished Abel Zelatov, the Senators star right-winger, with a bodycheck that put Zee out for over a month. The video shows the post-game scrum with McCormick, taken in the Flames locker room, clips from his three goals and the hit, and then another scrum with the Senators captain, Shane Parsons, mouthing off about poor refereeing and goons.

I don't tell Guy—"Call me Guy. We like to keep it informal

here at the radio station, Griffin"—that I've actually watched this video about twenty times before. Nathan McCormick is one of my favorite players.

"Okay, you've seen the clip," says Guy. "Now, I want you to write a news blast that captures the main points for the listener. Imagine they haven't seen it, so you've got to present it to a listener in a nutshell."

"Okay. You mean a script? As if someone is reading it on the news?"

He nods. "That's it. Copy for a newscast. Pick out the main points, audio clips, too, and report. Can you do that?"

Can I do that? Um ... yes.

I nod and he opens a new Word doc on his laptop and pushes it over to me. "Okay. Let's see what you've got. Thirty minutes." And then he pushes his chair back and walks out, leaving me alone in his closet-office.

There's a moment—just a moment—when I look at the blank page and freeze. But that always happens. Words are my thing. Well, next to hockey, of course. I'm always taking crap from Jake and the other guys because I read the *Citizen* cover to cover every day. And the Saturday *Globe*. Books. Magazines. Blogs. And I write stuff. The guys know my notebook is good for some Sci-Fi escape on road trips to tournaments. They tend to pass over the non-fiction, current events commentary stuff, though

33

(as demonstrated by my Ottawa teammate Evan: "What's this crap, Griff?").

So, a blank page and a "Let's see what you've got" is like giving me a chance to take shots with the Stanley Cup Champions. Let me at it.

Guy comes back a half-hour later, but I've been done for about five minutes. I spent the last few minutes looking around his office at some of the stuff he has tacked up on the walls. Framed photos of him with various athletes, unknown to me, so probably local. Hockey players, a group of golfers—maybe a charity fundraiser, because I'm pretty sure that's a former Senators player in one of them. There's one of Nathan McCormick in a suit, looking awkward, with Guy and another guy, who, when I look more closely, I recognize as a young Josh Drouin. The photo appears to have been taken in this radio station. Interesting. Just as I'm starting a search on my phone— "Josh Drouin, Nathan McCormick, The Legend, Glenavon"— Guy returns.

"Done yet?"

I nod at the laptop. "Yup. Hope it's okay."

He sits down and pulls the laptop over, and I can tell from his grin—maybe smirk is a better word—he's pretty sure he's about to read a bunch of amateur crap. And it's very possible it is a bunch of amateur crap, but I just hope it's good enough.

He reads it out loud, as if he's doing a newscast, which is a bit awkward. I wish he'd just read it silently and let me know. Whatever. I'm starting to think Guy Martin is a bit of a showman.

"Calgary Flames defenseman Nathan McCormick scored a hat trick in a 7-4 win over the Ottawa Senators on Saturday night at the Canadian Tire Centre, but it was McCormick's hit on Senators star left-winger Abel Zelatov that drew the most attention after the game.

[insert audio clip here: McCormick]

"'I think it was a clean hit. He was crossing the blue line and looking back for the pass and, yeah, I was there, and he just saw me at the last minute. No knee-on-knee, no crosscheck. I just hit him and he fell awkwardly, I guess.'

"McCormick was not assessed a penalty on the play, and Senators captain Shane Parsons saw it differently.

[insert audio clip here: Parsons]

"'How the refs missed that, I don't know. Zee tried to sidestep to avoid him at the last minute and McCormick went high, like he always does.'

"Zelatov had to be helped from the ice and did not return. Reports from the Senators say he'll miss at least two weeks with an upper body injury.

"The loss was the Senators fourth in a row. They'll be looking

to rebound against the New York Rangers on Saturday night at the Canadian Tire Centre."

Guy looks up after he finishes reading and doesn't say anything for a moment. Just looks at me, thinking.

"Yeah, I made that 'next game' part up," I say, a bit unsure because I can't read the look on his face. Did I screw it up? "I figured that was probably something you'd do in a real newscast." Shut up, Griffin. "And the clips—inserting the audio clips—I transcribed them. But maybe I got that wrong?"

"You got it right, kid," he says finally. Nods at me.

I unclench my hands (which I didn't know were clenched) and breathe again. "Great. Good. Thanks."

"Hockey's your game?" he asks, and I nod. "Fine. How about you come with me to the Moose pre-season game at the arena next week, on Friday night, and you can see what kind of stuff we do. Sound good?"

"Sounds great," I nod. Wait. "Stuff. What exactly do you mean by stuff?"

"I'll be doing a wrap-up for the Saturday newscasts, and you can help. Record the scrum. And maybe you could do some social media?" He raises his eyebrows at me, asking, *Do you know how to do social media?*

"Yeah, great. So, should I meet you there?"

"I'll send you the details and we can meet up at the arena ...

how's that? We can watch the warm-up and I can introduce you to the unbelievably ass-freezing media bench at the Glenavon Community Arena. Wear your woollies, kid."

He grins at me then and reaches over to shake my hand. "Welcome aboard, Griffin. You've just become part of the 99.1 Sports Department."

"Thanks so much. I can't wait to get started."

"Hey, Elise!"

I met Elise, the station manager, when I arrived. Friendly, teacher-like, youngish—as in, younger than my parents. She's out there talking to some of the volunteers. Now she sticks her head through the doorway, smiles at me, and raises her eyebrows at Guy.

"All done? We good?"

"Add Griffin Tardiff to the staff directory," says Guy. "I think we've got another Josh Drouin here."

And he grins at me and nods. "You're part of The Legend now, kid.

GIRLS

I do not understand girls.

I should, because I have a reasonably cool mother and two somewhat unique older sisters, who have launched themselves into the world and are doing great things, like teaching kids about science and technology, and advocating for answers to climate change, (yes, my sisters are busy, committed, smart, and a bit scary, actually.) You'd think I'd have some inside knowledge of how the female brain works.

But I'm constantly confused.

This one's on me, though: I totally forgot that I said I'd head home—as in home to Ottawa—to hang out with Blair on Friday night. There's a social thing at my old school, and I was going to get one of my parents to drive me, stay at Jake's, hang out with everyone, and maybe even tell them about my exciting new life in Glenavon.

Which would also mean listening to them tell me all the things I'm missing back home, but, whatever ... I'd be with my people again.

Only ... my upcoming gig at The Legend kind of pushed everything out of my head, and now it's after supper on Thursday night and I'm on the phone with Blair and she's pissed. Apologies and reasonable explanation are not working.

"But you said you would be coming home," she says. One thing about Blair, she doesn't whine. She just says stuff straight up. Straight up with a lot of unsaid words. "And now you're not."

Unsaid: *I can't trust you if you can break promises like this.*

"I know. I'm sorry." We've been going around in circles. This is about the fifth time I've apologized and tried to explain.

"So, this hockey radio thing, or whatever is going on there, is more important than coming home to see your friends? See me? Is that what you're saying?"

Unsaid: *Did you meet someone new? That's it, isn't it?*

"No, of course not. But right now, I'm new at this, and the guy told me I need to work on Friday night, and I'm trying to make a good impression. You know how it is."

"Yes, Griffin. I know. It's all about hockey, right? And it's the dream job in broadcasting. *Small town* broadcasting."

Ouch. She's the all-star setter on the senior girls volleyball team, so I've seen her on the court when she sets up a perfect spike

39

that Becky or Jas misses. Seen her face, with that expression of disgust, before she tucks it away and becomes the good teammate again. She's a tiger, Blair. Sometimes she goes a bit too feral, but I have to say she always comes back. It's just getting her to come back, that's the mystery. I never know if I'm saying the right thing.

"Yeah, hockey and broadcasting. You know me." Silence. I soften it up a bit. "Look, Blair, there's just so much to get used to here. Everything's new and I don't even want to be here. You know that. Next weekend, I promise."

It works. I just flubbed the spike, but she's going to be a good teammate and set me up for a second chance.

"Oh, well," she says. It sounds as if she's smiling. For real smiling. "I guess if you have to bail on us, then you have to. Next weekend, right? Promise?"

All of a sudden, everything is sweetness and light. What? How? It's like a switch flicks somewhere in her brain, and she changes direction so fast I can't keep up.

"Promise," I say, thinking, *Oh, man, don't let Guy Martin sign me up for something next weekend, too ...*

"I miss you." And when she gets mushy, I know it's time to bail.

"I miss you, too."

And then that switch flicks again and suddenly she's Busy Social Girl: "Well, gotta run. Meeting up with some people at Orleans. Later, okay?"

"Sure. Okay."

"Bye!" Big smooching noise and then the red button and she's disconnected.

As I hold the phone and try to figure out what just happened, I see there's a text from Jake, replying to my message about having to cancel out of our weekend.

Np. Let me know how it goes. Next stop HNIC?

That's Jake. No problem and a plug for Hockey Night in Canada. This guy gets me, which is why he's my best friend. I text back:

Cold media bench at small town arena. No HNIC yet

And then another message from him:

Blair pissed?

Oh, yeah. My boy Jake gets it, all right.

Yup

She'll be OK. You'll be famous one day and she'll forgive you

I send him the thumbs up. He might be right, but you never know. I mean, *girls*, right?

I'm sitting at my desk during all this phoning and texting, watching but not really watching the street out front, seeing Blair's face, mostly, and Jake's. And our school gym, where all my friends will be getting together tomorrow night to kick off the new school year without me.

Actually, I'm having faint second thoughts. Maybe I *should* tell Guy Martin there's this thing I forgot about, postpone my first assignment for The Legend. I mean, it's pre-season, right? And it is pretty short notice. And I could always play the "My parents reminded me that I have a commitment in Ottawa on Friday night" card (which is not completely untrue. My mother did in fact remind me of this previous engagement, but I could tell she was actually pretty happy I was staying in Glenavon to pursue an interesting school-related media opportunity, instead of her having to drive me up to Ottawa, where I would get into all sorts of unsupervised fun with my man Jake and The Girlfriend. Not sure Mom approves of Blair completely ... just saying.)

Yes, I could do that. I think about it while gazing out the window without seeing anything out there. But I'm not going to. This radio station gig has me buzzing, and I know myself well enough to know that's a buzz I should listen to. Blair is Blair, and she's unpredictable and hard to figure out. Jake gets it, though. Jake knows me.

And then my eyes focus on something on the sidewalk in front of our house. Someone.

That kid, Noah. Holding a hockey stick and standing there, watching our front door.

I watch for a few seconds, thinking he might just go away if I don't come out. Of course, he might be brave and come ring the doorbell, too. Whatever. The kid is weird but he's harmless. And he's holding the hockey stick I gave him.

I head downstairs.

"Hey, Noah," I say, coming out the front door and down the steps of the porch toward him. And now I see he's not alone. In the time it took me to walk downstairs, Rosie has turned up as well. She's standing there in her black jeans and T-shirt and a long, dark green sweater-cape thing, one hand on his shoulder. They're talking to each other, but as soon as I come out the door and down the front walk, they stop and look at me. Identical hazel eyes. It's a bit unnerving.

"Hi, Rosie." I nod at her and she nods back without speaking. Maybe she doesn't appreciate the "Rosie" thing. But that's what the kids at school call her, and Noah, of course.

"Hi, Griffin!" Noah is happy to see me, at least. "I was wondering ..." he starts, and Rosie interrupts him. Gently, true, but still, she cuts him off before he can roll out the request.

"Now, Noah, I told you, you can't just wander down here and expect him—expect Griffin—to want to play hockey whenever you want to, right?" She doesn't look at me while she's talking. "It's a school night, and people have homework and things to do. Right? So, come on now. We should go back home."

"Do you have homework, Griffin?" Noah asks.

I look at Rosie and she's looking right back at me.

43

I mean, does she not want her little brother hanging around with me, the unknown guy down the street?

Or is it about hockey? Not wanting to tempt the kid because they can't afford for him to play?

Or is there some family thing going on that means Noah should be staying closer to home, and not wandering off down the street like this, carrying a hockey stick and standing on the sidewalk in front of people's houses?

No idea. I wish I could ask her, but the answer to every one of those questions could be awkward, so I don't.

But something, some thought, some emotion, flits across her face for a moment. Those intense eyes, unblinking. Her mouth— it's a small, perfectly shaped mouth, no lipstick (details I notice because Blair's is the complete opposite), lips pressed together just a bit, as if she's holding back words.

I take a chance on hearing what she's trying to tell me and hope I get it right.

"Hey, it's no problem. Come on, Noah." I nod over at the driveway. "I'll get my stick and we can take some shots, okay? Homework can wait."

He runs up the driveway now, bouncing on his feet and tapping the too-big hockey stick on the pavement. Honestly, the kid's face—pure joy.

"Yay! Let's play, Griffin! Can we use the net?"

"Sure, I'll get the net, too."

Rosie is still standing there, and we exchange a look before I turn back up the driveway. She doesn't say anything to me, but she pulls her drapey sweater around her and crosses her arms to hold it tight, nods at me, and then looks at her brother.

"I'll be back in a while, Noah. Not too long, okay?"

"'K, Rosie. Not too soon, okay?"

"Okay."

And then, without looking at me again, she turns and walks back down the sidewalk.

But just before she turns, I get a glimpse of her face. Her mouth is curved up in a slight smile. Which means I must have got it right.

ON THE JOB WITH GUY

Guy Martin was right. It's freezing on the media bench at the Glenavon Community Arena.

But honestly, I don't feel the cold, because he has me running up and down the stairs most of the game, taking photos of action on the ice (through the glass, using my phone) and in the stands. Stuff we use on The Legend's social media feed. This early exhibition hockey game seems to be the only thing going on in this town on Friday night, so he says we have *carte blanche*.

"Just have fun with it," he says. "Soak up the atmosphere."

He was late meeting me for the warm-up. I stand in the foyer of the arena for about twenty minutes, thinking I must have got the time wrong, before I finally spot him through the glass doors, taking a last drag on a cigarette and tossing it away. He ambles in and catches sight of me.

"Sorry, Griffin. Held up over supper," he says.

My mother gave me the lecture about dressing for The Job, so I'm wearing my black jeans and Gloucester hockey jacket (yes, complete with championship and MVP crests), which is both warm and a bit show-off-y. Don't care. And clearly it doesn't matter, because Guy is wearing jeans and a The Legend 99.1FM official jacket with a Prescott Moose crest as well. We definitely have the hockey media look covered. He takes in my jacket, the crests, and nods.

"Nice. Okay, let's go. Hope you're in good shape, because this media bench is not for the weak."

We have to walk past the entrance to the dressing rooms, and guys are milling around, some in partial uniform, some in street clothes. Players. Coaches. A couple of these guys call out to Guy, some in French, some in English, all along the same lines. *Back at it, eh? Nice to see you here on time for once.* Only with a lot of swear words thrown in.

He answers the same way, laughs it off. I can tell he loves it.

The media bench is more like a couple of tables on an overhanging platform just above the stands. Well, three flights above the stands. I'm fine—it's my arm that hurts, not my legs—but Guy's definitely puffing by the time we get up top. Of course, cigarettes will do that to you, too.

"Home sweet home," he says as we come to the section high over the penalty box, looking across at the team benches. "Take a seat."

He pulls out a chair and thunks his laptop case down on the table as he sits down. So, I sit next to him and look around.

It feels like home. Okay, yes, I've never been up in the press box, the media bench, whatever, but when I look around, I see all the things as familiar to me as my own house.

The ice—blinding white, with those lines and circles that mean everything when you're out there playing. When you're watching, too, I guess. And the white boards with their ads and logos. And scuff marks from pucks, sticks, players' equipment. Probably the occasional face, too. The benches, grubby and perfect. And the stands, which are just rows of cement with lengths of wood, like benches, painted to jazz them up a bit. Still really hard and really cold. And up high, around the walls, banners. I see a couple of Glenavon High School championships, as well as three ringette banners from recent years. And the Prescott Moose, of course. Finalists last year. Champions a few times in the past. The classic electronic scoreboard and timeclock. And a whole lot of dull concrete walls filling the background.

In other words, typical small-town arena.

Guy catches me sitting there at the table, grinning.

"Ready to get to work?"

"Yeah, sure." I nod. "Just tell me what you want me to do."

He does. The night goes by in fast motion, starting with the warm-up. I snap phone photos of both teams and text them to Guy, who puts out a pre-game Twitter post. Next, it's fans streaming in. I run into a few familiar faces—Brad, Murph, Mike. Mr. Dunbar is there with a couple of young kids and says hi. Then, opening face-off.

Good photos. Come back to bench

Two flights of cement stairs, one of creaking metal.

"These are good, Griff. See what I do with them?"

He brings up the radio station Twitter feed on his laptop and shows me his posts. Hashtags, team tags, snappy captions.

"We don't use Instagram for sports so much," he says. "And definitely not Facebook during games. Algorithm's way too weird for anything going on in real time. I leave that up to Elise."

I don't tell him I already know all this social media stuff. And more, probably. But he seems pretty old-school and, after all, this is kind of small-scale social media for a small-scale news outlet, so I just keep my mouth shut. *You're not working for Hockey Night in Canada yet, Griffin.*

"Okay, your turn," he says, somewhere around the start of the third period. He's been typing notes into his laptop, getting his game recap ready, I guess. He doesn't seem to want to venture too far from the media bench.

The Moose are leading 5-1 and the fans are loud, so he sends me out to catch some fan photos—"Cute kids are good. Ask their parents for permission"—and when I get back, I text him the photos, and he gives me his phone to post them myself, since I don't have account passwords yet. First, a little photo editing and cropping, then the caption with team handles and hashtags. (Brad and Murph tried to get me to take their picture, but I told them they weren't cute enough.) Guy doesn't even watch me, his eyes on his computer or the ice. I could be checking out his email and photo stash if I wanted. Which I don't.

I hand him the phone when I've drafted it and hold my breath.

@TheLegend99.1

Fans showing @PrescottMoose some love vs @Kemptville Aggies in preseason action tonight at Glenavon Arena #Moose IsLoose #TheLegendSports #BestFans

A group of three photos shows fans with Moose gear, signs. The main photo is a little kid with a moose hat. The hat is awesome, and the kid himself is pretty cute.

"Nice. Nice. That's Cedric Lavallée," says Guy, nodding at the draft. "His grandfather drives the Zamboni here. Good choice." And he hits the Tweet button to send it out into the world.

On the ice, the Moose score again, and the place gets crazy loud for a moment.

I pick up my phone and navigate to Twitter. Yup, there it is. And I get that hit you get when you see the numbers of Likes and Retweets ring up. People are reacting to my tweet on The Legend's feed.

My tweet.

I can't help grinning. Best community service job ever.

"Come on, Griff. Now you get to experience the post-game scrum," says Guy beside me, and I snap back to the cold media bench and an arena of fans cheering and clapping, because the Prescott Moose have just won their pre-season game. "You can snap a couple of photos of me talking to one of the players, so I can put them up with a link to our audio."

"Right ... okay," I say. Post-game scrum sounds so cool. I'm already thinking of all the stuff I'll have to tell my parents later tonight. I'll have to text Jake, too. He'll love this. And I should probably text Blair, just to keep things good with her.

Guy picks up his laptop case and is heading for the stairs, and then he turns to me, questioning. "How old are you, anyway?"

"Sixteen."

He pulls his jacket collar up around his neck and grins.

"Too bad, Griff. No post-game beers at The Commercial for you."

"I guess not, no."

"I could sneak you in, if you want," he squints at me. "I know people." *Wait, what?* And then he grins. "Nah. Just messing with you."

We both laugh it off as I follow him down the stairs, and I'm thinking, *Yeah, I probably won't be telling my parents about that part.*

THE GIRL WHO DRAWS

Rosie's sitting by herself, in the far corner.

I see her as soon as I come into the library on Monday morning during my spare. She's in one of the beanbag chairs over by the window, just on the edge of the little reading hangout area that's set up between one set of shelves and another. She's a little apart from the couch and the other floppy chairs, which are currently occupied by some whispering Grade 9's with their laptops open. They're either doing an unusually fun school project or surfing inappropriately, I can't tell, but they're not paying any attention to the girl in the corner with her head bent over a sketchbook.

She sits perfectly still, except for one hand drifting like waves over the page, letting the pencil find its way. That's what it looks like—as if the pencil is doing the work and she's watching. She's in the zone, I can tell. I know about zones.

"Hey, Griff, you going to work on our math problems?" Suddenly, Brad is there, with Murph trailing along beside him, as always. They're so unexpectedly loud that I'm about to shush them.

She hears us and looks up. The pencil has stopped moving.

"Uh ... yeah. That's what I was thinking," I say, nodding at the guys and then looking back at her.

Now she's packing her sketchbook and pencil into her shoulder bag, rising from the beanbag chair, not looking at us.

"Good. You're smarter than we are, so you can help us. Let's go find a spot at the tables over here," Brad says, and he moves off with Murph in tow.

"Okay." I nod when I see where they're headed.

She has to pass us to get to the door. The guys ignore her, but I try to catch her eye.

"Hi, Rosie."

"Hi."

And she slips past me.

"You and Rosie?" asks Brad as I find the worktable and sit down. He snorts and Murph does the same.

"What?"

"Nothing." Meaningful shrug. "She's just not your type."

"My type? What's my type?"

Brad leans back, thinking. Although I'm not sure Brad is actually capable of intelligent thought.

"One of the smart girls. Athletic, or at least knows something about sports. Wears real clothes that have actual colors and maybe some style. Long hair."

He doesn't know it, but he just described Blair perfectly.

"Yeah, well, I just know her because she's a neighbor." Time to shut this down. The idea of Brad Scott sending Griffin-and-Rosie innuendoes around school doesn't sound like a great idea. "She has this little brother. I'm coaching him on some hockey stuff."

"Right." Brad's smirking at Murph. "The little brother."

My strategy for getting people to shut up is to stop talking. I look at Brad with a blank expression on my face for a moment, until he notices that I'm not saying anything one way or the other—which is a lot like saying, "You can think what you want"—and then I reach for my pack and my math books and get to work.

They do the same, groaning. Rosie and her brother are forgotten. For now.

NEXT ASSIGNMENT

"You're kidding, right?" Once again, Blair is not happy.

It's been a bad day. The pain woke me up again through the night. Clearly, I shouldn't have taken on Murph in one-on-one hoops in gym class Tuesday. That guy is big and loves pushing the body contact fouls. Also, he seemed to know exactly how to force me to overwork my left arm.

I still beat him, of course. (Man, he's slow. And not just in his moves, either. Slow thinker. No anticipation. I wonder what he's like in net.) But I'm paying the price with a couple of sleepless nights.

And now my Saturday plans with Blair have just been exploded by an email from Elise Rogers.

Great job with social media on Friday night. Guy says you were an ace. I'm thinking about giving you the account login to

make it easier for you on-site. Would you be interested? Also,
I wondered if you could join Guy on Saturday morning at the
arena to do a short report and some social media on the minor
hockey start-up. Little kids. Just an hour on Saturday morning
between 9–10? Let me know. Thanks!

I reply immediately with a big yes, of course. No-brainer. Especially the part about the account login, which means they must really want me around, doing stuff for them.

This is good news, because as we stood outside the arena on Friday night, talking, while I waited for Dad to pick me up, Guy didn't say much about future assignments at The Legend. He did talk about the town: "Lived here all my life. Yeah, it's small, but that works for me." And himself: "Once I dreamed of moving into big-time sports reporting. Still think about it, but this small-town stuff is pretty important, too, you know?"

But he's vague about next steps as Dad pulls up in front of us.

"Nice work tonight, Griffin. Elise or I will be in touch about the next gig. Okay? 'Night."

So, I've been watching all week for something. I was giving them until today, Thursday. If I hadn't heard anything by today, I was going to email Elise. Ask her if I did okay at the Moose game and see if they had any plans for me coming up.

"You don't get anything if you don't ask for it," Mom said

to me last night, as I stewed out loud about why I haven't heard anything. "Just email them."

"I will—I'm just trying not to be obnoxious."

"Griffin." My mother looks up from the kitchen table, where she's got her notes spread out for this course she's developing. She's in teacher mode. "There is nothing obnoxious about showing initiative."

I shrug. Yeah, heard that one before. So she switches to mother mode.

"And you could never be obnoxious, anyway. It's one of your gifts. Inherited from me, of course."

But I didn't have to get obnoxious, because this email arrived, and now I'm back on The Legend beat, this time with some audio, too.

And Blair is pissed.

"Come *on*, Griffin. Again? You're canceling again?"

"I know, I know. I'm sorry."

"You're not sorry. You're loving it." Of course, she's right. I can hear her smiling, because she knows me so well.

"I'm sorry, but I can still come up on Saturday afternoon sometime. We can still hang out. That's what we were going to do anyway, right?"

"Except that you were supposed to be here Friday night for the party at Melissa's. And now you can't be here, which means I have to go alone. And everyone will ask me why."

She's trying to make it sound as if that's going to be a problem, but it won't be. I know. The volleyball team and the bravest of their friends, male and female, playing this weird volleyball-hybrid game the girls invented in Melissa's backyard. There's holding allowed. And body contact. It's bizarre, and it's played only when Melissa's parents aren't home.

"Yeah, you'll have to go alone and crush them all with your aggressive V-ball skills. You know you love that." Now it's my turn. "And you know I suck at that game."

"Too short." We say it at the same time, and now we're laughing, and I know it's going to be okay.

"Saturday afternoon, as soon as I'm done," I say. "My mom has to come up to the college to pick something up, so she's going to drop me at your place. I'm all yours for the rest of Saturday."

"Promise? Will Jake be tagging along?"

"Only if you want him to." Jake and I are a bit of a package deal, and she knows it.

"Well, we'll see."

If I were a sighing-in-relief kind of guy, I would be sighing in relief. But for now, I just listen as she fills me in on life at school, the stuff that goes on in those familiar hallways, gym, cafeteria. Some of the stupid stuff, the good stuff. Teachers, the annoying ones and the good ones. I let her talk, missing it a lot.

But I'm also thinking about Saturday morning and hanging out with Guy at the arena, and little kids and their parents and coaches, little kids getting ready for the hockey season, maybe for the first time in their lives. And me helping to get it out on the radio, getting the message out on social media.

Blair talks and I manage to say stuff. But I'm not really listening.

REGISTRATION DAY

It was a scene of excitement and controlled chaos this morning at the Glenavon Arena as the Glenavon Minor Hockey Association held its annual league registration for the upcoming season.

"We expect somewhere around three hundred kids to register for hockey this season, about two hundred of those under the age of ten. That's maybe a hundred more kids than we had last season."

That's the word from Don McPherson, league chair and parent of ten-year-old Jackson, eight-year-old Sasha, and six-year-old Emily, all of whom will be on the ice this season, wearing the Glenavon blue and yellow, as they compete against teams in the larger Prescott and Area Minor Hockey Association. McPherson says the local league is going strong, with its reputation for emphasizing skills development as well as fun. He's been fielding calls from parents from neighboring associations who are looking for a less competitive environment for their kids.

"That's our philosophy here, and we all buy into it. Parents, coaches, officials, and the kids themselves. Build the skills and have fun. Yeah, there's competition, for sure there is, and yeah, the kids play to win. But if it's not fun, what's the point?"

Fun was definitely on the agenda as kids took turns at the shooting range, tried on skates at the skate exchange, and posed with Prescott Moose captain Beckham LeMay in the Selfie Corner. And yes, the ice was full of skaters, too, trying out their blades for the first time this season under the watchful eye of the officiating team, many of whom are students from Glenavon Collegiate Institute and École secondaire de St. Gregoire, like St. Gregoire Grade 9 student Matt Lemieux, who also plays with a house league team during the winter.

"I don't know, I just like it. It's exercise. Like, I think when you're reffing, you're actually kind of learning more about the game, too. And yeah, it's a job, too, so you get paid. And the kids are pretty good. And the parents. Nobody yells at me or anything. It's just fun. I mean, look at all these kids, just having fun."

If Saturday morning's registration excitement is anything to go by, young hockey players in Glenavon are going to have a great season, and that, says Don McPherson, is all anybody wants.

"Yeah, registration day is always kind of nuts, but we expect that. And it's worth it to keep our minor hockey league thriving. Kids are getting exercise, fans are coming out to cheer them on, everybody's having fun. I mean, what else is there, right?"

This is Griffin Tardiff at the Glenavon Arena for The Legend 99.1.

I think for a minute Mom might be about to drive off the road. She's drifting seriously toward the right shoulder and I look over at her. Her eyes are on the road, but her mouth is open in a "wow" kind of way.

"Mom?" Some ad for snow tires comes on, and I reach forward to turn the volume down. Yes, we're on our way to Ottawa, listening to The Legend 99.1, just before we drift out of broadcast range, and they just played my report after the noon news.

"Oh, Griffin, that was fantastic!" She straightens the wheel out and looks over at me. "Honestly, that was so professional, so good. Where did you learn to do that?"

No idea, to be honest. It all came pretty naturally.

Well, pretty naturally once I recovered from a moment of panic when Elise's email arrived, telling me that Guy couldn't make it.

"Oh-oh." I was staring at my phone just as Dad turned into the parking lot at the arena.

"What's up?" He looked over at me. "Wrong day? Wrong arena?"

"No. Elise says I'm on my own." I look back at him. "Guy Martin can't make it this morning."

I'm sure he saw the panic on my face, but he just asked: "Do you know what to do?"

"Yeah, I guess so." Interviews. Record interviews. Take some photos.

"You've got this, Griff." My dad's pretty unflappable. Everyone says that's something I inherited from him, but right then, at that moment, I'm pretty sure it didn't show.

But I do it. I walk in and introduce myself to Mr. McPherson (as instructed by Elise), get a couple of interviews and take some photos for social media (and remember to ask for permission from parents). Then back to the studio—thanks, Dad, since I haven't got around to driving lessons yet—to write and record the report and fit in the clips. Honestly, it just seemed to flow, like I'd been doing this forever.

So, to answer my mother's question:

"No idea. It all just happened."

"Well, it happened like magic, then. That was fantastic."

"Thanks, Mom."

We drive for a moment and I can see her glancing at me out of the corner of her eye.

"What is it, Griffin?"

My mother knows me very well.

So I tell her. About the interview I didn't include in the story. The one with a coach named Al Blaine, an older guy whose kids are all grown up now and not playing in the league anymore, but who loves the game and working with kids, and who told me about the big problem that nobody talks about.

"Yeah, this is great," he said, waving a hand around at all the excitement. "And I don't want to be a downer here. But there's still too many kids who miss out, you know? It's just so bloody expensive to play this game. To buy equipment, to pay registration fees, to travel, if your team gets into a tournament somewhere. Gas, hotels, meals, registration. Kids grow and need new equipment in the middle of the season."

He shrugs and shakes his head. "It's expensive, bottom line. And not all families in our region can afford to be part of this. There are programs out there, of course. JumpStart being one of them. But some families don't feel comfortable, you know? Asking for help? And, I don't know, it eats at me. It's just a shame."

And as he was speaking, I felt myself nodding, because ...

"Do you play?"

"Nah. My mom won't let me because it's too expensive."

Noah, who thinks the most exciting thing in the world is taking shots on my driveway. Walking home with one of my old sticks and a tennis ball. That's all I could think about as Mr. Blaine was talking.

"Listen to this." And I pull out my phone and play the interview for Mom.

When it's over, I wait for her to say something, but she doesn't. She's nodding, though.

"Remember Greg Butler?" I ask her.

Greg Butler, gifted athlete at my middle school. This guy could play any sport, do anything with a ball, a puck. Track and field. Greg was the fastest runner I ever saw. But there were four younger kids in the family, and a dad who was raising them alone, running a gas station, and there was no money or space in his life for expensive sports like hockey.

"I do remember Greg," Mom says.

It's a perfect fall day, sunny, leaves starting to change in the patches of bush along the highway. The Ottawa River sparkles into sight every now and then, farms, cows, fields of browning corn still standing. And way in the distance, the first glimpse of the hills, the Gatineaux.

I'm going to see my girlfriend. My best friend, too. I just did a great job on my first real solo assignment for The Legend. ("Great job, Griffin!" Elise told me as Pete, the technician, lined the file up in the queue for broadcasting. "You're a natural!") I got all my homework done last night and I'm free from obligations until Monday morning. My arm isn't even hurting right now. I should be celebrating.

But, but … what?

Mom and I drive for a while in silence, and then she says:

"So, Griffin? What are you going to do about it?"

Yeah, my mom knows me very well.

WEEKEND

We come up for air when we hear the back door open.

"Shit, I didn't expect them home so soon," whispers Blair, bouncing off the couch—off the couch and me, actually—and smoothing her hair back into a ponytail. "Get it together, quick."

So I do. Grab my shirt and pull it on over my T-shirt. Right, pull the T-shirt back down, too. Run my hands through my messed-up hair. Pick the cushions up off the floor and toss them on the couch.

"Hi, Mom," Blair calls out with impressively fake boredom. "Griff's here. We're watching baseball."

Thank goodness we left the TV on. Sounds of packages being dropped on the kitchen table, a few words of conversation between Blair's mom and sister, and footsteps. By the time her mother appears at the family room door, I've managed to catch my breath and there we are, snuggled cozily on the couch, watching the afternoon game between the Jays and Orioles. No sign that five minutes ago we were doing a bit more than snuggling.

"Well, hello, Griffin. How lovely to see you," says Mrs. Wheeler. "Home for the weekend?"

"Mom, Griff's 'home' is Glenavon now," says Blair. "Remember?"

Mrs. Wheeler gives me a sympathetic look. She hears the same tone that I do, the one that says Blair hasn't forgiven me completely for—well, for leaving. As if I had any control over it.

"Hi, Mrs. Wheeler. Hi, Jess." I nod at her little sister, who's already got a Gatorade and granola bar to match the mussed-up hair and red face of a twelve-year-old on her way home from a hockey game. "How d'you do?"

Jess's eyes are on the TV. "Won. Scored a goal."

Jake arrives to pick me up an hour or so later, just in time, actually, because since our interrupted afternoon hook-up on the couch, Blair has been slowly turning toward the dark side. It's like sitting pressed up against a tree trunk. Hard, all knots and sharp branches, no reaction when I trail a finger across her cheek. She's not pouty or anything, but it's like she's flipped a switch and decided I'm not there.

Yeah, I guess she hates that I'm not around as part of the school social scene anymore, part of the entourage.

And it probably didn't help that when Mrs. Wheeler asked

me about my new house and school in Glenavon, I found myself telling her in detail about my gig reporting for The Legend this morning, and (why oh why oh why?) this little kid down the street who comes and takes shots with me, and his sister ...

Yeah. That was a mistake.

"Big fail," says Jake as we're walking to his house, me carrying my backpack with overnight stuff and trying to describe the change of temperature that Blair sometimes surprises me with. "The radio stuff—she doesn't want to hear about anything that you're enjoying while you're away, right? And bud, come on, you don't mention other girls."

"She just a girl in my class. A neighbor. It's her little brother who's the story here."

Jake shakes his head at me. But he's grinning, too. "Blair is Blair. If she's not in charge, she's gonna take it out on somebody."

True. So true. Everything was fine until that conversation with her mother about life away from Ottawa.

"She misses you, that's all," says Jake.

"Yeah, I know."

I miss her, too. Why can't she see that?

"Come on. By the time she comes over for the game tonight, you guys will be back to the cute couple everyone knows and loves, right?"

Sens and Leafs tonight, pre-season game viewing party in

Jake's rec room with the guys from the team and some of the girls, too. (I'm staying over and getting a ride back to Glenavon tomorrow with my sister Bella, who's coming for Sunday dinner to check out the new house.) There's going to be lots of unhealthy junk food and loud color commentary, and probably a pool on who wins, who scores, and best play of the night. And lots of hockey talk, team talk. Lots of talk that won't actually involve me anymore, but I'm okay with that because these guys are still my team.

And that's exactly what happens. Supper with Jake's family—crazy, loud, full of arguments about politics, some cooking show on TV, and whether the Yankees are going to win the World Series (Jake's dad is a serious Yankees fan, in the minority, because Jake and his brothers and sister have allegiances all over major-league baseball).

Then everybody starts to arrive and we take over the rec room. They leave a space on the couch for Blair and me, which is awkward, because Blair hasn't shown up.

The text comes at the end of the first period. I miss it, actually, because I'm not paying attention to my phone at all. I'm watching the between-periods interview with Josh Drouin and one of the Sens players. I notice how relaxed Drouin is, how relevant his questions are, how they sound natural, flowing from what the guy says. A smooth send-off—"Thanks for this, Tyler.

Good luck in the second."—as if they're just guys talking along the boards, not being broadcast across the country live.

Josh Drouin, who started at The Legend, mentored by Guy Martin. Who people in Glenavon actually call "The Legend." So cool.

"He started at the same radio station I'm working at," I tell the guys, who start making Hockey Night in Canada jokes. They've heard about my radio gig from Jake, and start in on a debate about who the best sports broadcaster is. My name isn't mentioned, of course. It's in the middle of this that I glance at my phone.

Sorry can't make it tonight

Okay, she must be really pissed at me.

I'll come get you. I miss you

Long pause, then ...

Ok. Ten minutes

So I do. Walk over and meet her on the sidewalk in front of her house, and then a slow, quiet walk back. Quiet but okay. She's thawing again, her hand entwined in mine. And so it's a good night with lots of laughs, and us wrapped up together on the corner of Jake's couch. Our friends. And hockey. When I walk her home later, we spend a good twenty minutes in the shadow of the lilac tree beside her garage, and it's as if the afternoon chill thing never happened.

"I do not understand girls," I tell Jake later, when I'm bunked down in a sleeping bag on the air mattress in his bedroom.

"That's why I don't have a girlfriend."

"Smart."

"Yup. I'm way smarter than you.

"True."

We're quiet for a minute and my brain should be slowing down, but it's not.

"Hey, Jake, remember Greg Butler?"

"Greg Butler? Sure. What about him?"

"That kid I was telling you about. Noah. The little kid who comes over to take shots? He reminds me of Greg. He's a weird little kid, but he can shoot, you know? He's good with the stick." Jake doesn't say anything, and I go on. "And his mom can't pay for him to play hockey."

Another pause, and I think maybe Jake has drifted off. But he hasn't.

"This is the kid with the sister?"

"Yeah, but she's not ..."

"Help the kid," he says. And then he adds: "Just don't tell Blair."

He starts snoring shortly after, and I lie there for a while, staring at the ceiling and thinking about Noah. And Blair. And, yes, the sister, too.

The pain wakes me up two hours later.

RETURN

Thanks to somebody's dad who is in the Oldtimers league, the guys were able to get ice time at the local arena for an hour on Sunday morning, so Jake gets his older brother Harrison to drive us over.

"Why am I even doing this?" I ask, when Jake hustles me out the door after a quick breakfast of toast and juice. "I don't even have skates with me."

The last time I was on skates, the ambulance guys had to peel them off me. And the last thing I feel like doing is standing at the boards in a cold arena, watching the guys play shinny. But Jake just grins and hauls me out of the car and into the front foyer where one of our teammates, Evan, is standing there with his gear.

"All yours," he says, holding up a pair of Bauers. "I just got new ones."

I had forgotten that Evan and I wear the same size. I look at him, then at Jake. This is a set-up, clearly.

"No, I can't."

"Yeah, you can," says Jake. "Come on."

He's already heading down the hallway toward the dressing rooms, and Evan has basically dumped the skates into my arms and is following him, grinning. They think this is funny.

I don't think it's funny. I haven't been on skates for over six months. Dr. Fitzpatrick probably wouldn't think this is funny, either, especially if I told him about waking up last night. Again.

But, yes, I follow them, carrying the skates. And yes, I sit down on the bench and kick off my running shoes, and slip my feet into Evan's Bauers ... and oh, man, it's like sliding into soft sand as I tighten the laces.

Something crashes to the floor in front of me. A helmet, tossed over by Evan's dad, one of the three older guys there. "You'll need this, Griff," he says.

They loan me a stick because they want me to play shinny with them, but I say no. I just want to skate. I just want to feel the ice again.

So, while the guys follow the puck around—no equipment, just sweats and gloves and helmets—I skate slowly in the spaces where they aren't. Feel my edges, hear the blades on the ice, let the cold air rush into my face, washing away that memory of the boards and the pain and guys with the stretcher. I just skate until the Zamboni guy honks his horn and we have to get off.

Oh, man. I miss this so much.

EMAIL

Hi Griff,

Sorry I couldn't be there on Saturday morning for the minor hockey registration. Heard your report and it was great. You're a natural.

GCI hockey team tryouts are Wednesday after school this week. Interested in being the point man on coverage for the school team? I'm busy with the Moose and some other stuff. I've copied Elise here. She's on board.

If you're interested, can you drop into the station Monday afternoon after school so we can make plans? Let me know.

Guy

I read it over a few times to make sure I've got it right.

"Wow."

"Good news?" Bella is driving but she glances over, smiling, eyebrows raised. My tone of voice must have said it all.

"Yeah, good news. They want me to cover the school hockey team for the radio station." Brad and the guys will be in heaven if this works out.

"That's fantastic, Griff!"

Bella picked me up at Blair's this afternoon. Yes, a few hours at Blair's on Sunday afternoon seemed like a good idea after our hot-and-cold-and-hot-again Saturday. Good call. Blair was back to normal (normal? What's "normal" for Blair?) when Bella arrived and honked at me from the driveway to wrap it up.

"Get a room, you two!" she yelled from the car window.

My sister Bella has her own apartment in Ottawa, and a job doing educational outreach for the science and technology museum. She and Mom and Dad like to have conversations around the dinner table about curriculum tie-ins and classroom resources, and she's always on the road, visiting schools or arranging speakers for conferences. There's ten years between us, and two years between her and our older sister, Claire. Yes, I was the family afterthought and my sisters never let me forget it. *Everything was running so smoothly and then you came along to mess it up, Griff ...*

I know they don't mean it. We're cool, my sisters and me. But they're sort of in a different world—I'm still in high school and there's Bella with her education stuff, like Mom and Dad, and

Claire doing environment-related policy work on Parliament Hill and raising little Andra. Yes, Claire has a husband, too—Denis. A good guy, works in finance. Really funny and sharp. But he doesn't mind joining me on the driveway with sticks and net and tennis ball, either.

I'm lucky, when it comes to family, and I know it.

"This is like real radio work, isn't it?" Bella says, as we cruise down the highway toward Glenavon and Sunday dinner, some CBC book show playing softly in the background. "You and this placement?"

"Yup. It sure feels real."

"Mom texted me about that report you did yesterday—the minor hockey thing? She was pretty excited. There may have been tears."

We laugh about that. Our mother is generally pretty cool in front of us, but we all know she can transform into mushy mama bear sometimes. Okay, fierce mama bear, too. Dad's the even-keeled quiet one, the one who calms everything down, makes you feel like it's all going to be okay. But Mom, yeah, we can count on Mom to be the one clapping and maybe yelling the loudest when we need it. Sometimes when we don't.

"Yeah, I know it's just a community service thing for school but, man, it feels so real," I say. "Like it could actually lead somewhere, you know?"

She does know, and we talk about it a bit more before settling back into our own thoughts. The radio show continues—some author talking about his depressing book on the melting Arctic ice cap—but it hardly registers with me.

Because in my head, I'm already at the arena, interviewing Coach Bedard or Mike or Brad about the upcoming season. Sending out tweets about scores, upcoming games. Taking photos of practice. Maybe I'll get to go on the team bus to games. It could happen, couldn't it? Like a real reporter?

I reply to Guy's email with a c.c. to Elise:

Hi Guy,

Thanks for this offer to cover the school hockey team. It sounds great to me. I'll stop by the station tomorrow after school and we can talk about it.

Thanks again.

Griffin

My head is so full of me and The Legend 99.1 and my budding career as a Josh Drouin-clone sports reporter, that it's not until we turn onto our street that I remember Noah.

Noah with his hero-worshipping, and his effective wrist shot, and his *My mom won't let me because it's too expensive.*

"Here we are," says Bella as we pull into the driveway. She

leans over the steering wheel, peering at the house. "Not bad at all. Come on, Griff. Mom said there will be pie."

I grab my stuff from the back seat and follow her up the porch steps. Take a glance down the street, in case there's any sign of a little kid with a hockey stick.

No one in sight.

SAFE HOUSE

The doorbell rings. Not just once, but three times. Four times. As if someone is jamming their thumb on it over and over.

It's Monday night. I'm doing math problems in front of the TV, because my parents have gone out to some meet-and-greet at the college, and they're not here to tell me what an ineffective way multitasking is to do homework. I don't know. I think algebra and pre-season NHL hockey work very well together.

I will admit, I'm finding it hard to concentrate, though. No, not because of the TV. Because my head is still full of my conversation with Guy and Elise after school this afternoon.

First, the Twitter and Instagram accounts—and a pile of papers I had to sign, agreeing to The Legend 99.1's social media rules and expectations; also hastily assembled references from my dad and Mr. Pike, the principal of my school in Ottawa, with assurances that I'm a responsible person who will not go rogue.

Sign-in and password given to me on pain of death.

"You can imagine how we would be concerned if, say, one of your hockey buddies got hold of this," says Elise.

I think she's being unfair to my hockey buddies, who aren't even that social media savvy, but I nod because I kind of know what she's talking about. Open access to the radio station's accounts would be a train wreck in the hands of someone like Brad, or worse, Murph. Elise has nothing to fear from me, and I'm pretty sure she knows it. Griffin is responsible. Story of my life.

"So, you can be at the arena on Wednesday afternoon after school for tryouts?" Guy asks me.

"Yeah, no problem." I'm already seeing the drills that coaches use to separate the skill levels, already imagining Brad swooping around like the Big Man because, let's face it, he is. I want to see Mike in action, though, and Murph, too. Maybe he's a fantastic goalie after all ...

They talk a bit about timing and logistics of filing reports—one or two a week—as well as the possibility of getting me on the team bus for some of the away games.

"Details we'll sort out as we go along," Guy says. "I've got some guidelines for you, templates and stuff. And you can ask me anything, anytime, okay?"

"We'll see how it goes, okay, Griffin?" Elise is the boss and she's playing it safe. I'm okay with that.

"Whatever you guys think," I nod. I know I'm going to be on the team bus. I'm so going to make that happen.

So that's where I am—not really paying attention to this fairly easy algebra problem, while picturing road trips on a school bus—when the doorbell rings. And rings.

First instinct is to ignore it, because I'm not great with people selling stuff at the door. And who do I know who would be ringing our doorbell at eight o'clock on a Monday night? Exactly. No one.

Whoever is out there is not just politely ringing the doorbell, though. They're holding it down and doing multiple bursts. I think I hear a thump on the door as well.

My Spidey senses are tingling because this is weird. I have a fleeting thought—*Wish Mom and Dad were here*—and then I stand up because I know I'm being a wuss. *Just answer the damn door, Griffin.*

And when I do, Noah is standing there.

"Rosie said to come here," he says before I even react, and it's such a crazy thing to say that I stand there in a cannot-process-this fog, until I realize that the kid's jacket is undone and falling off him, and he's breathless and shivering, and his eyes are wide with—what?—terror?

Rosie said to come here ...

"Come on in, bud. Let's get you inside."

I guide him in with one hand, while holding the outside door open and taking a quick glance up and down the street. Don't know what I'm looking for—maybe someone chasing him? Or a dog? Or a gang with knives? There's nothing. Just the empty sidewalk, dusky and lit at intervals by the streetlights. The street looks shut down for the night.

"Okay, let's get your jacket off. Here." I help him with it and realize the kid is almost vibrating. Fear? Cold?

No, it's fear. His lips are shaking, eyes wide as he stares at me.

"She said to come here if I was worried."

"It's okay, Noah. You're safe here." I put my arm around his skinny shoulders and guide him into the family room, but not even the hockey game and my math homework catch his interest. "Here, sit here." I have to disentangle him a bit because he's pressed into my side, but he sits on the couch, arms wrapped tightly around himself, and I sit on the table so I can look at him. "So, what's going on, bud? Why are you scared?"

He gulps a few times and, while he does, I'm thinking beyond what he's going to say, thinking I should call Rosie, call his house, and tell his mother where he is. I mean, a little kid running down the street at this hour? Shouldn't he be in bed by now? And do I even know his mother's name to find the phone number?

"The man is at our house," he says.

85

Okay, I was not expecting that.

"What man?" I have a terrible feeling about this. Is this going to get weird? Or dangerous?

"The guy who comes to visit my mother sometimes."

Oh, yeah, this is so getting weird. But the kid is obviously really shaken up, so I plough on.

"What guy?"

Noah gulps again, but he's calming down a bit now.

"The guy. Her friend. He comes over and they drink stuff and laugh and talk. And they were getting really loud, and I thought I heard my mom crying, so I left, because Rosie told me if I was scared when she wasn't home, I should go and see you. Go to Mrs. Miller next door or go to your house, she told me. And Mrs. Miller's lights weren't on. So, I went out the back door where they wouldn't notice, and I ran here."

He stares at me, eyes wide.

"It was getting dark," he says, and then his face just crumples and he starts to cry, as if the whole thing has just caught up to him.

Oh, man. So many thoughts are going through my head right now, as I visualize some weird scene with the mother and her boyfriend having a drinking party in their living room, escalating into raised voices and arguments and maybe even violence, and this kid hearing it all as he cowers in his room, shaking. Creeping down the hallway, sneaking into the kitchen and out the back door. Then running through the dark to get to my house, because his sister told him that's a safe place to go.

And where is Rosie, anyway?

I move over to the couch and put my arm around his shoulders, pull him in close for what I hope passes for a comforting hug. His hands are over his face and he turns and buries himself in my side. And cries.

"You're okay, Noah. You're safe. We'll figure this out, don't worry. You're okay now."

Crying Kids 101. I don't know what else to do.

But while he cries, I'm quickly dealing with the thoughts racing through my head.

First, where's Rosie, and why did she tell him to come "to Griffin's house" if he was scared?

Second, is Mrs. Courville in danger? Who is this man?

Third, where's my phone? I need to call my parents.

Noah is calming down a bit now, sniffling more than crying, and still pressed against my side, under my arm. I'm about to ask him a few more questions, see if I can find out more, when the doorbell rings once, and he jumps.

"Don't let him in," he says. Whimpers. He's actually hurting my ribs a bit with how hard he's pressing into me.

"Hey, it's okay." I'm trying to disentangle myself. "You stay here, okay? Stay here with the hockey game. I'm going to answer the door, but you're safe, okay? I won't let anyone in."

He lets me stand up and I grab the old knitted afghan from the back of the couch behind him and tuck him up in it because, man, the kid has started to shiver again.

The doorbell rings again and I give him a pat. "Just stay here. I'll be right back."

I'm thinking it has to be his mom, and I sort of prepare myself for a conversation—with a possibly drunk woman that I don't know—about her runaway son. But it's not.

It's Rosie. Eyes wide and clearly trying to keep it together. Geez, these two kids and their panic mode.

"Is he here? Is Noah here?" She's already stepping in, staring at me.

I don't even have time to nod and say yes, when we hear Noah yelling her name from the family room, and then he's there, flinging himself at his sister, trailing the afghan. She bends and wraps him in a hug, and Noah's crying again. Rosie makes soothing noises, mostly using the same lines that I used.

"It's all right, Noah. I'm here. It's all okay. Good for you, coming to Griffin's house. I'm sorry that happened but you're okay now. It's okay. Let's go home—come on."

She straightens up and looks at him, her hands still resting on his shoulders. "It's okay to go home, I promise."

"But is he still there?"

"No, he left. I got home and he left—it's okay."

"Mom's okay?"

"Mom's fine. She's tired. She's going to bed, but she wants to see you first." And then Rosie smiles at him and pushes his hair off his forehead. "And look at you, up past your bedtime. Come on. Get your jacket and we'll go home, and I'll read you a story and you can say goodnight to Mom, okay?"

"Okay." Noah is tired, or maybe just emptied out after this traumatic adventure.

I grab his jacket off the stair railing and hand it to him, and Rosie helps him put it on.

"Bye, Griffin," he says. His lower lip shakes a bit and I'm afraid the tears are going to start again. "Thank you."

"No problem, bud," I say and give his skinny little shoulder a squeeze. "Glad I could help."

She guides him toward the door; they're almost out, and then she looks at me.

"Thank you."

"You're welcome, but ..." I start to say. I mean, come on, I need some explanation.

And she knows it. She stops me with a warning shake of her head.

"Tomorrow. See you at school tomorrow. Okay?"

And I see that she's holding it all together for the kid, but she's about to crack open, too. I'm more than a little worried for her, though. She said the man was gone. She said her mother was heading off to bed. That's good, right? But still ...

"You're sure everything's okay?"

I mean "safe" of course, and she doesn't smile, exactly, but she softens, nods at me. Understands.

"Yes. Everything's okay now." She steps out the door, pushing Noah ahead of her and not looking at me.

"Okay, then." It sounds lame and I say it to the back of her head.

They start to step off the front porch, but then she turns back and looks at me.

"Please don't tell your parents," she says, quickly, quietly, maybe so that Noah won't hear. "Tomorrow. I'll tell you tomorrow."

And before I can say anything, she turns away and leads her brother back home, arm tight around his shoulders.

AND, NOTHING

I keep an eye out for her on my morning walk to school, but no sign of her on sidewalks in either direction. I wonder if maybe she walks Noah to the elementary school first, which would take her off the direct route to GCI. Or maybe their mom does that?

Last night's confusing revelations about their mother drinking with some loud man at home have stirred up imagined scenes that belong on the latest intense TV cop drama. *Two kids, huddling in fear, the mother under the influence of some bad dude, a potential crime scene ...*

Rosie asked me not to tell my parents, and I didn't. But, man, I really wanted to.

They came home just as the game was wrapping up, and there's my math homework, still open on the table.

"Griffin," my mom looks at me. The *look.*

"Done. Honest," I say. "Hours ago."

I don't tell her it took me a while to settle back down into the world of algebra, though, because my head was full of Noah's face, the feel of his shivering little shoulders. Rosie's voice: *"Tomorrow. I'll tell you tomorrow."*

And now tomorrow is today.

No sign of her at her locker, which is in the same hallway as mine, but about three classrooms away. I don't even know if any of these unknown girls currently standing in the vicinity would know where she is, since she seems to hang out mostly solo. Also, asking random girls about someone is a bit like standing on a chair and yelling "Yeah, me and Rosie!"—which isn't something I want to do ... so ... no.

I run into Brad at his locker—"Watch the game?" "Yeah, if they don't get a decent goalie, they're toast."—and we go into homeroom together.

She's already there, head down, leaning on her elbows with hands hiding her face, headphones on. She doesn't even look up when I come in, and stopping by her desk to start a conversation, especially with Brad still doing his color commentary of the game, seems like a bad idea, so I go sit down at my desk at the back.

Either she's avoiding me or ... yeah, she's avoiding me.

Mr. Dunbar reminds us that it's extended homeroom today, so he has a brilliant plan to go around the room and give everyone a chance to say a few things about our community service placements. Oh, great. Show and Tell time.

"Just a quick update, guys. Where you're working, something about your role there. Just a couple of sentences, okay?"

A silent groan goes around the room, because nobody really wants to get up and talk about themselves in front of the class.

"Okay, let's just go in order by rows. Patrick? You first. Up to the front, please."

We hear reports about the local daycare, the elementary school, a gymnastics club, several farms, my gig at the radio station (although I don't mention the coverage of the school team yet, because Brad's head would probably explode), a garden center, town hall. And then it's Rosie.

She goes up to the front ("It's good practice for you," Mr. Dunbar insists at the start. "Talking in front of a group." No, it's hell for most people, Mr. Dunbar ... just saying) and turns to face us.

"I'm working at the Avonlea Seniors Lodge. I'm helping the administrator, Mrs. Campbell, with a media project to record the residents' stories for a sort of historical record that the museum is going to put on display."

Ah. I wasn't wrong about the tech-savvy side of Rosie, obviously.

She's done, and she's about to head back to her seat, when Mr. Dunbar stops her.

"So interesting, Rose. And such an important project. I was hearing about it from my great-uncle Archie. He lives at Avonlea."

Rosie nods politely and slips into her seat. Clearly, she does not crave the spotlight and isn't interested in keeping the conversation going. But oh, yes, Mr. Dunbar is very interested.

"You know," he says, in a voice that shows he's having a brainwave. A brilliant plan. "I'm thinking that there might be a chance for a connection here," he says.

And he's looking at me.

"You know, maybe getting these stories on The Legend. Wouldn't that be great, Griffin? And Rose? A radio show that shares some of these stories and memories—history, really—from some of our community's seniors?"

He looks back and forth at Rosie and me, and neither of us has an answer for him, but I can already hear the stirring among our classmates.

Suckers. Dunbar just hooked you up.

And then Rosie says, "No."

Even Dunbar is surprised at the fierceness in her voice. There's an awkward pause as he frowns, gets close to speaking again—and then I jump in.

"I don't know, either," I say, because I can tell from the way she just wrapped her arms around herself, a lot like the way Noah did last night, that she needs rescuing. "I mean, I'm doing mostly sports stuff, and not regular programming. And from what I see there, they have a really full program at The Legend already." I'm skating here. No idea what I'm talking about. "And every programming decision has to go through the station manager and a board, so I'm not sure this is big enough, you know? Or even something we could suggest there?"

Okay, I'm starting to ramble a bit, but I just want to shut this down.

"Oh, thanks, Griffin. I see," says Dunbar. Does he? Does he see that I'm skating here, trying to make it okay for Rosie, whose shoulders are hunched, the hand that I can see clutching her upper arm tightly. "Well, just a thought."

He gives Rosie a look that says he knows there's more going on here than he understands, but he backs off. Looks at me and nods, as if he knows that I know there's more going on here, too.

"Okay. You're on the ground there, Griffin, so you're probably right. Right, Richard? You next."

And when homeroom is over, Rosie is out that door so fast, I don't even have time to call her name.

TRYOUTS

I don't exactly have my nose pressed up against the glass—okay, maybe I do—but I'm down at ice level, watching the guys do beep drills and thinking, *man, there are some fast skaters out there.* Brad being one of them, which I didn't expect.

"They look good."

Guy Martin appears beside me, wearing his The Legend 99.1 jacket.

"Yeah, there's some speed out there," I say, still a bit surprised at Brad.

"They had a great season last year," Guy says. "Made it into regional playoffs. They only lost a couple of decent seniors at graduation, so the core's still here." He nods at me. "We need to keep our eyes on this team. Could be a good season."

I like the "we" part. It feels good to be part of a team again.

Actually, that might be the worst part of this injury—well, no, the worst part is that it's taking so long to heal, and it still hurts a lot—but the team part is killing me, too. The no-team part, I mean. Being left out, left behind.

Because I've always been on a team, since the earliest memories of Timbits hockey skills at the local arena with Jake, the two of us already miles ahead of the other kids, even at age four. There we were, skating around pylons, begging the coaches to let us shoot pucks.

"Skills first, guys, just be patient. We'll get there."

We weren't patient. Jake's dad made a rink in their backyard, something you can do in Ottawa because winter arrives in November and stays until at least April. We were out there every day, every night. His dad had to put lights up because it was too dark for us to see what we were doing. Jake and I were a team before we were even on a team.

"You miss it," says Guy beside me, and I realize he's been watching me, and it must be written all over my face how hard this is.

"Yeah."

"Injuries suck. What happened?"

"Smashed my arm, humerus, really high up."

"Into the boards?"

"Yup. I saw it coming and I couldn't do a thing. Tried to turn,

97

but too late." I don't like to relive that moment and conversations like this don't help.

"Still hurts?"

I nod. No need to describe the regular nightly wake-up calls.

"Could've been worse, you know. Head. Neck. Or take it in the shoulder and you're screwed for life," he says. "Speaking from experience."

I look over at him, curious.

"Yup," he says. "I was one of those guys. High school team right here, then into the system, major junior—and Bam. One very, very bad check from a monster defenseman the size of a barn door, and an exploded shoulder and a concussion, and that was it for my NHL dreams."

Okay, so I don't have NHL dreams. I know I'm way too small to take the heat there, and probably not talented enough, either, but this is the nightmare story that every athlete dreads: the injury that killed the dream.

"Sucks," I say. Inadequate, but all I can come up with.

"Sucks." He nods.

Yes, the two radio guys are standing at the glass, sounding a bit pathetic. Brad and Mike suddenly roar by on the other side of the glass, chasing a puck up the boards. They don't even see us.

"But you know, then I got into the media program at Carleton, got a chance to stay around the game. Do some fun stuff, still be part of the scene." He turns and nods at me. "It's all good. You just have to take advantage of the opportunities when they present themselves, right? Like this gig at The Legend."

He's in pep-talk mode, probably for my benefit. Time to change the topic, and I know exactly where to go.

"Hey, I wanted to ask you about a photo in your office. The one with Nathan McCormick? And Josh Drouin? Just wondering when that was taken."

The guys are scrimmaging now, skates and sticks cracking the air and the thud of contact between bodies and boards. We both watch for a moment.

"That was just after Nathan signed with Calgary," Guy says. "He went to school around here, did you know? Hillside Academy, up in Brick Hill. Got tucked away there for a while after that thing at the world juniors."

I nod, remembering "that thing at the world juniors" where McCormick beat up a Swedish player and got suspended for months. And then disappeared for a while until the big hockey federations figured out what to do with him.

"So, Josh was studying at Carleton, J-school, and I was able to set up an interview for him with Nathan just after he got drafted, before he left for Calgary." He turns to me. "Josh did the same kind of thing here at The Legend that you're doing.

And he did some of his internships with us, too, once he was at university. Good training ground, you know?"

"Well, he's sure doing great now. He's all over the hockey broadcasts."

"Yup. Taught him everything he knows," Guy laughs. "Seen enough here? I can give you a lift home, if you're ready."

He drives a sporty suv with an Ottawa Senators frame around the back license plate. Black. Very shiny, although we all know no one wastes time on polishing once the snow flies. It has all the toys—screen full of apps, dash cam, probably heated everything.

"Okay, where to?" he asks once we're strapped in.

"Sixty-six Stanley."

"Stanley?" He glances over at me as he's pulling out of the parking space.

"Yeah. Up near Higginson," I say, wondering what's so interesting about Stanley.

"Right." Eyes back on the road. Nothing, I guess.

The radio isn't tuned to The Legend. Instead, it's some sports talk station full of heated discussion about the Ottawa Senators upcoming season and predictions of failure. Guy loves it, talks back to the announcers. We laugh at the one announcer, who tries to convince us that they're going to trade the goalie (a goalie who was in the Vezina voting last year, so, yeah, no.)

Guy knows exactly where to go. We turn off the main road, down a hill, and then make the turn onto Stanley.

"Thanks for this," I say, as we drive the few blocks toward my house at the other end. "Number 66."

"No problem. Just up here?"

"Yeah, the gray brick, with the white Toyota in the driveway." Mom's home.

Actually, Mom's there, I realize, as we pull into the driveway. She's at the front door, talking to—yes, Noah. Noah and his hockey stick.

She looks up as we pull in, trying to identify us, and then catches sight of me in the passenger seat and waves, says something to Noah. *Here's Griffin, now you can play hockey,* or something. And then she's looking confused, because Noah is taking the porch stairs like he just got called home for supper.

"Hey, Noah," I say, as I'm getting out of the car, but Noah just gives me this little smile and says, "Gotta go home," and then he's trotting and then running down the street, back the way we just came.

"That is the weirdest kid," I say to Guy, who is standing beside the car, watching Noah and his hockey stick disappear down the street.

"Yeah, I know the family," says Guy, and he turns back, shakes his head. "Weird kid, for sure. Does he come here often?"

"We take shots on the driveway. He told me he can't play hockey 'cause his mom says they can't afford it."

"Yeah, I can believe that," Guy says, and then he waves up at my mom, who is still standing at the door. "Hi, Mrs. Tardiff. Guy Martin from the radio station."

"So nice to meet you," calls Mom. "I'd come down and shake your hand but I'm in sock feet, so you just get a wave. Sorry." *Oh, Mom.*

But Guy just laughs. "No worries." And then he says to me, "You were saying, the kid, and not being able to play hockey. You've talked to him about it?"

"Just a bit. I mean, he's just a little kid but, I don't know, it bugs me," I say, wondering if I should play him that clip from Mr. Blaine. "I was thinking maybe there was something I could do. Maybe for kids like Noah, not just him. You know, promote some of the programs in place to help families with costs—JumpStart or one of those. Or advertise the equipment exchange more. Something." I shrug. I sound like a do-gooder.

But Guy nods. "Not a bad idea. Let's talk about it sometime." He thumps the roof of the car and gives me a wave. "But right now, I gotta get going. Back to the station. You've probably got homework. And a mom who expects you to set the table, I bet." He definitely has my mom figured out.

"Thanks for the ride."

"No problem. Get working on an intro to the hockey season, maybe grab an interview with Brad Scott—he'll probably be assistant captain this year. We can get a clip in on the weekend roundup maybe, okay?"

"Sure, okay."

"I'm off to get ready for the Moose. They're over in Kemptville next week to kick off the season, and I've got some prep to do."

"Okay, thanks again."

"The Legends at work, hockey style." He points at me and laughs, gets back into the car, waves once more as he heads back down the empty street.

I watch his taillights disappear around the curve of the road. No sign of Noah and his hockey stick.

DOCTOR

"Does the pain still wake you up?" Dr. Fitzpatrick asks without looking at me. He's sitting at his computer, squinting at scans. This is an improvement, because for the past few minutes, he's been moving my arm around and taking note of my efforts not to show how bad that feels.

It's Friday afternoon and I got off school early, so Mom could drive me up to Ottawa for this appointment. I'm meeting up with Jake and the guys at the rink, staying at Jake's tonight, then meeting up with Blair tomorrow afternoon. I was looking forward to the weekend, but this appointment—not so much. Dr. Fitzpatrick doesn't mess around, which is why he starts with the pain question.

"Not as much as it used to."

He turns and looks at me with a *Let's try that again, and this time give me the straight answer* look.

"No, really," I say. Cool. Not letting his look get to me. "It used to be every night. Now it's just once a week, maybe."

Mom shifts in the chair beside me but doesn't say anything. I know she's thinking, *Why didn't you tell me this?*

Dr. Fitzpatrick looks back at his screen and nods. "And what are you doing for activities? No hockey, I hope?"

"No hockey." Okay, no need to mention being on the ice with the guys a few weeks ago, because that wasn't really hockey, was it? "Gym class. Basketball, shooting hoops. Some ball hockey on the driveway. The resistance bands and weights the physio gave me."

"Increased resistance? Increased weights?"

"Yup."

"And?"

I shrug. "It feels pretty good."

There's a pause and he looks over at me again. "But there's still some stiffness and pain."

"Yeah." No point lying. "There's still some stiffness and pain."

"Let's give it another month, Griff. Come back in November and we'll take another look."

It's not as if I was suddenly going to go try out for the team, although the thought had actually crossed my mind, stiff upper arm or not. But waiting another month to have him say, "You're healthy, you're healed," is not what I was hoping to hear.

He knows it. He's been there since the beginning, the sports-specialist surgeon they called in as I lay drugged and groaning on the hospital bed, getting prepped for the operating room, and now he gives me a sympathetic grin and a shrug.

"You'll know when you're ready, Griff. You'll have your full range of motion back; the stiffness will be gone. You won't be waking up with pain."

"But why is it taking so long?" It takes a lot of effort to keep the catch out of my throat, and I'm pretty sure I sound like an eight-year-old. A whining eight-year-old. My mom shifts again, but she doesn't say anything, thank goodness.

"Because you had a traumatic injury. Because you're sixteen and your bones are still growing." He pauses and shrugs again. Looks at Mom and then me. "And because I'm very cautious with athletes who have potential to do big things in their sport. I don't want this to be the moment you look back on and say, 'Yes, I could have made it to the NHL, but the stupid doctor let me go back too early ...'"

Guy Martin and his exploded shoulder, and *that was it for my NHL dreams.*

"I really don't think I'm NHL material," I say. "I just miss it, that's all."

Dr. Fitzpatrick nods. I wonder how many athletes he's heard that from.

"Griff, I understand," he says. "And you'll be back there, maybe even later this season. Certainly in time for a full year next season. In the meantime, keep up with the strength and resistance exercises. Do your cardio, your stretching. You can even skate. But no equipment, no body contact. Got it?"

"Got it." He's a good guy, and I know he understands why I can't make eye contact all of a sudden. "Thanks."

Mom doesn't say anything as we drive over to the arena, where I'm going to meet Jake and the guys after their practice. Friday afternoon ice time for my old school team, and I get to watch. Oh, yay.

"I'll see you Sunday at Bella's, okay?" she says as we pull up at the arena door.

"'K. Bye."

I climb out with my backpack and I'm about to shut the door, but she leans over.

"Griff." Catches my eye and makes me look at her. "You'll be back on the ice. Stronger than ever."

"I know. I know. It's just ..."

"It's just that you miss it, buddy." She doesn't use that little-kid name for me very often, so I know she's feeling it. "But in the meantime, you're working on being The Legend, right? And that's not so bad."

That makes me laugh, breaks up the warm fuzzies, which is fine.

"True." The Legend. Yeah, that's me. "Thanks, Mom. See you Sunday."

"Hey! Behave yourself!"

But I've already shut the car door, while giving her a grin and a wave, signing off without actually acknowledging her instructions. It's an art.

I walk into the arena, push open the doors to the rink, and breathe in the sweet aroma of ice, concrete, and well-used hockey equipment. I drop my pack and stand at the glass behind the net, trying to ignore the dull ache in my arm thanks to Dr. Fitzpatrick and his "just checking your range of motion" examination. Yeah, I ignore the pain and watch my guys doing the only thing I really want to be doing.

And it just sucks.

MALL

Blair is lounging in one of the armchairs in the fancy section of the food court, one hand wrapped around a large double-double, the other holding her phone and thumb-scrolling. Skinny jeans, school hoodie with the Wildcats logo, long blonde hair swept up in that weird half-ponytail thing she does. Her eyes are on her screen, and I can see her lashes against her high cheekbones.

She hasn't seen me yet, so I just stand there for a minute at the edge of the food court, watching her. It's not weird to do that when it's your girlfriend, right? Also, she wouldn't mind, anyway—she's used to being looked at, the center of attention. She's not a show-off, Blair. She's not one of those mean girls, or a lightweight in the brains department, either. She's just one of those people who knows where she wants to go and isn't afraid to cut through the crap to get there.

She looks up and sees me. A beat. The only thing that moves

is her mouth, curving up in a slow smile. I just wait, then:

"Get over here," she calls out, loud enough that heads turn. She doesn't even care.

Yeah, she's pretty great.

We have about ten minutes to ourselves before Jake and Evan show up, and I spend most of it watching her, while she tells me about last night's volleyball team-bonding sleepover at somebody's house. Mani-pedis. Binge-watching that Netflix series. The new girl who transferred in from some school in Kanata and has fit right in. Team stuff. Girl stuff. I just watch her and nod. I love watching her talk.

"Oh, crap, here's the Dream Team," she says, as somebody tackles me from behind. Evan, of course.

"Shit!" I can't help myself. His hands are digging into my shoulders and my arm is crying out for mercy, thanks to Dr. Fitzpatrick and yesterday afternoon's fun range-of-motion manipulations.

"Oh, geez, sorry!" Evan immediately backs off. "Sorry, man. I forgot about the doctor thing."

I'm rubbing my arm, trying not to let it show that the pain actually made me feel a bit sick there for a second. As if I was suddenly transported back to that moment when the boards came up to meet me. I swear I can smell that other guy's equipment, hear his grunt and the animal sound I made as my arm shattered.

I take a breath. "No worries. It's okay. Getting better."

Maybe if I say it enough, I'll believe it.

"So, you guys can't entertain yourselves?" Blair asks, directing her boss-girl look at Jake and Evan, who are now leaning on the back of my chair, hanging over me. "Griffin and I were actually having a nice time. You know? Just the two of us?"

This is an ongoing conversation. The boys on our team, the girls on her team, some of the couples that have formed, the hanging out together. Alone. Together. I never know what Blair wants, because she so often seems to be all about the gang hang-out. And then she says something like this. As if being alone with me is all she wants. Girls. So confusing.

"Yeah, yeah," says Evan. "Whatever. Anyone hungry?" Which makes us all laugh because Evan is always hungry.

"I'm starving," says Blair. "Let's get some fries."

"Griffin!"

We all turn, startled.

It takes me a weird out-of-context moment to realize that Noah Courville is standing a few tables away with a huge smile on his face and his hand in the air, waving at me.

"Hey, Griffin!" In his other hand, he's holding a drink that's tipping a bit dangerously as he stands there, waving. He takes a step closer.

"Hi, Noah." I stand up, aware that Blair and the guys are

exchanging looks. *Who is this kid?* "Out shopping?"

Of course, he's out shopping. It's a mall. And he's not alone, because what eight-year-old kid would be shopping alone in a city mall on a Saturday afternoon?

Yup, Rosie's there, with her regular uniform of black jeans and long dark-green sweater-cape thing, a purple wool hat pulled down over her hair. And beside her is a woman—short brown-gray hair, jeans, and a red turtleneck—with the most exhausted expression on her face. This has to be their mother, I'm guessing. They're both holding coffees and random shopping bags, and frowning in my direction.

"Friends of yours?" Blair says without moving her lips.

"Yeah, shopping," says Noah, smiling at me as if this is the most fun ever, and making his way toward us.

I can see Rosie start to say something—"Noah, wait"—but that doesn't stop him. He's got the excited twitch going again, and I have to admit, as odd as this kid is, I can't help grinning at him. That drink is going overboard any minute.

And yes, I'm ignoring Blair.

"Come and meet my friends," I say to him as he arrives in front of us, beaming. Part of the gang. "This is Jake and Evan, my hockey teammates."

"Hi, Noah," says Jake, reaching over to shake his hand, which the kid fumbles a little. Must be new territory for him. "I hear from Griff you've got a mean wrist shot."

I'm not sure what hyperventilating looks like, but that might be what Noah's doing right now, smiling up at Jake, at me, at Evan, who nods at him. "Hey, Noah."

"And this is Blair, my girlfriend," I say, directing his attention to the chair opposite, where Blair-my-girlfriend is lounging.

"Hi." She gives Noah the regal nod and smile, and then I see her look over his head at Rosie, standing back among the tables in the food court. A glance at Rosie, a glance at me, then back to Noah. "Having fun shopping?"

Yeah, Blair is doing some thinking, I can tell.

"Oh, yeah, I got Senators pajamas," he tells Blair.

"Cool. Griffin has Senators pajamas, too," she says.

Which is true, and Noah jumps on it. Another reason for him to fanboy me. (Although my mind is spinning through the reasons Blair would mention that. To impress the kid? A joke? A sly reference to seeing me in my pajamas, which I don't think she ever has, actually?)

"Do you? Cool!" Okay, the drink spills a bit at that, and I reach out to steady it.

"Careful, bud. Don't want to lose your juice, there."

"Here, Noah."

Rosie steps up and takes the cup from Noah, brushes the drips off the front of his jacket with her hand. She doesn't look at me, at us, and it's one big awkward moment—until someone else moves into the circle.

"You must be Griffin." Mrs. Courville has joined us now, and she nods at the boys and Blair. And then she smiles at me, which changes her face completely. "So nice to meet you at last." She has a soft voice, a tired voice. "I know we're neighbors, but we haven't had a chance to connect."

I wonder if she knows just how neighborly I've been. As in providing safe haven to her kid on the nights she's not paying attention.

"It's very kind of you to let Noah come and play ball hockey with you," she says. Okay, no mention of safe haven.

"It's fine. I enjoy it." She's an older version of her kids, only with dark circles under her eyes. I try not to think of her and some guy knocking back beers and getting into fights at the kitchen table. That kind of activity will take it out of you, for sure.

"Well, we won't interrupt you and your friends any longer," she says, and I see her switch into mom-mode, reach out and put a hand on Noah's shoulder. "Come on, Noah. We need to get going."

"Bye, Griffin." Noah looks up at me and then the others in turn. "Bye, Jake. Bye, Evan. Bye, Blair."

"Bye, bud," says Jake. "Maybe I'll be over at Griff's sometime and we can take shots together."

Maybe because he grew up in a big, loud family, Jake is one

of those guys who knows how to talk to little kids. Noah is so overwhelmed, he can't even find the words right away, so he nods about five times as his mother gently directs him away, and then he recovers.

"Sure! That would be great! See you, Jake! Bye, Griffin!"

Rosie has been standing silently next to me with her eyes on her brother, and she's about to turn away, too, but I stop her with a hand on her arm.

"Hey, meet my friends," I say. "Guys, this is Rose. We're in the same class at Glenavon."

"Hi, Rose. Poor you," says Jake. "Being stuck with this guy."

The expression on her face has been all *Let me out of here*, but she takes a deep breath and smiles at Jake and his little joke. "Yeah."

"Hi," says Evan.

"Hi," says Blair, waving one hand in greeting and taking a long sip of her coffee, her eyes on Rosie, and then sliding to me.

"Nice to meet you all. See you at school, Griffin," Rosie adds in my direction, before turning away and following her mother and brother through the tables toward the exit of the food court.

"Wow. Weird kids," says Blair then, but just quietly enough that I hope Rosie doesn't hear.

"Is this the kid you were telling me about?" Jake asks. "The one who reminded you of Greg Butler?"

I glance at him and nod.

"He's your number one fan, Griff. I thought the kid was going to piss himself," laughs Evan, and I have a sudden urge to cross-check him, so it's really a good thing I don't have a stick in my hands.

"Interesting kid," says Jake, catching my eye. "Interesting family."

"Yeah."

"Stuff going on there, I'd say."

And this is exactly why Jake and I are best friends. "Yeah. For sure."

"That girl is into you, Griff. You know that, right?" says Blair, and when I look over at her, ready to protest, I see her grinning. She's kidding. Of course she's kidding.

"Not a chance," I say. "Besides, I'm not available."

"Oh, barf," says Evan. "Okay, fries. Blair? Coming?"

"Oh, yeah, I'm in," and she launches herself out of her chair and follows Evan, stopping to give me a big *mwahhh* kiss on my neck on the way by.

Yes, I let her. Maybe I even like it. But then, as she and Evan walk off, laughing about me, I turn and look toward the food court exit.

The three of them move slowly. A unit. The little boy, still excitedly talking between the exhausted mother and the girl I can't figure out.

CONVERSATION OVERHEARD FROM A HALLWAY

"Great job, Griffin," says Elise. "If I didn't know better, I'd say you were in your third year in the Media Studies program at Carleton. This is really good work."

It's Monday afternoon and we're sitting at the computer in her little office at The Legend 99.1, listening to an audio clip I sent her, with a report on the Glenavon Collegiate Hawks hockey team and their upcoming season.

"Coach Bedard says he's really looking forward to tackling some unfinished business from last season's semifinal loss to the Lancaster CVI Lions." My voice sounds so weird through the little speakers of her computer. Actually, my voice sounds really weird to me in any of these reports, but I guess that's normal. At least, Elise says it is.

There's a clip from the coach, then another clip from the captain, a guy in Grade 12 named Philip Oswald, talking about "the great squad we have this year" and "we're going to give it our all" and "we just have to take it game by game." Philip has clearly been listening to those between-periods interviews that Josh Drouin does on TV. You have to hope his on-ice playmaking is more creative.

Then my voice again, giving the dates of the first game, which is on the road, and the first home game at the arena.

"Glenavon Hawks are looking forward to another great season, and their fans also have a lot to look forward to. This is Griffin Tardiff, at the Glenavon Community Arena, for The Legend 99.1."

Yeah, I think it's pretty good, too, but you can never tell when it's your own stuff, right? So it's great to have Elise nodding and smiling as she clicks the playback off.

"No kidding, we are so lucky to have you here on board," she says, swiveling her chair to smile at me. "We'll have to make sure you get the permission forms for traveling on the team bus." She makes a note in the notebook she carries around with her all the time. "Guy has traveled with the team before, but it's been a while since we had an intern as capable as you. I can't see why they'd mind. You must know some of the guys. I'll look into that and let you know. You'll probably have to get your parents to sign a permission form, if the school's athletic department goes for it." She shrugs. "Can't see why they wouldn't with someone like you, telling their stories and making them look good, right?"

Team bus. This just keeps getting better.

We chat a little more about school, about the team and my coverage.

"I saw that you got the passwords, right? For our Twitter and Instagram?"

"Yup. I put one thing out on the weekend, after that first report aired," I tell her, although I'm pretty sure she would have seen it. "I used a photo I took from behind the glass—that's okay, right?"

"Perfect. Just remember the rules about pictures of kids, right? You need parents' permission."

We cover a few more technical things, and then we wrap it up.

"I'm so glad this is working out," she says as I stand up. "Guy came up with the idea kind of at the last minute. Maybe remembering what a great experience we had with Josh all those years ago. You know Josh Drouin, right?"

"Oh, yeah, I know who he is."

"We call him The Legend around here, for obvious reasons," says Guy, who has appeared at the doorway. I wonder how long he's been standing there. There, or just outside the door, listening.

Now he nods at me. "Good report."

"Thanks." I grab my pack and head for the door, and he has to stand aside.

"Hey, Griff, I've got some ideas for that thing we were talking about. I'll email you," he says as I slip by.

That thing. That thing? He must see the confused look on my face.

"You know, the kids who can't afford to play hockey? Giving everyone a chance to get out on the ice? That thing?"

Right. Noah. That brief conversation in my driveway, when he drove me home last week after watching the tryouts. I'm not sure what he's planning to do with it, but since it was my idea, I guess he wants to make it a team thing. I'm good with that.

"Yeah, okay. Just email me or whatever." I nod at him, nod at Elise, who waves goodbye with a smile. "Bye."

Although I'd like to be focused on my conversation with Elise—team bus!—I'm actually distracted by Guy's final comment there, about hockey for everyone. It's been in my head. Noah's been in my head, especially after that unexpected encounter at the mall on Saturday, but I'm still vague about how to help the kid. And why is Guy getting all over this, anyway? He doesn't even know Noah. He wasn't there on registration day to hear Mr. Blaine's words.

Still mulling it over, I stop partway down the hallway to dig my earbuds out of my pack, and it's while I'm stopped there that I hear Guy speak to Elise, and I freeze, because his voice is weird.

"Okay, I'm here." Then he's inside her office. "What now?"

"You know what, Guy. You bailed on Saturday morning with Griffin. Okay, you had to go to Ottawa on personal business, fine. But then last Monday night." Elise's voice sounds tired. Like this is a conversation they've had before. I know that voice because it's the same voice my mom uses when she's telling Dad about the stupid decision made once again by some administrator at the college.

"Look, they were expecting you to show up and you didn't. They had asked specifically for someone from the radio station, and I assigned you. You didn't show up."

"Come on, Elise. It was just another cheque presentation. To the Seniors Center. That girl from *The Tribune* was there and sent me a photo. You saw it. I got it up on the socials." He sounds like he's talking to a child. My mom would have him on his knees if he talked to her like that.

Also, I know I shouldn't be standing here listening. I should be long gone, down the hallway, out the door, on my way home.

But I'm not. I'm standing here listening to a meeting between my two sort-of bosses. And now I'm afraid if I start to move, they'll hear me. Yeah, but what if Guy suddenly steps out and sees me?

Bad situation, Griffin. But I don't move.

"We pay you to do a job, Guy. It's not just sports here, you know." Elise isn't intimidated, and I have a feeling this isn't the first time they've had this kind of conversation. "We're the community radio station. *Community*, right?"

Silence.

"Look, I know you're enjoying this internship thing with Griffin, and it's going great, honestly, but you have a job to do, outside of the sports department, and that means sometimes doing crap jobs, like saying nice things about another cheque presentation. Right?"

Big sigh. Then a theatrical groan. Then, "Yeah. I know. It was just going to be so fucking boring."

Wow. Didn't expect the swearing. Elise doesn't seem shocked, though.

"I know. But it's the job, and I can't justify keeping you on staff and paying you if you don't do the job—so just do it, all right?"

A sigh, a pause. I imagine them looking at each other.

"Yeah. Okay, boss."

I decide that as soon as they start talking again, I'm going to hustle as quietly as possible down the hallway.

"Where were you, anyway?" Elise asks. Okay, I'm ready to tiptoe away toward the main door at the end of the hallway. Really, I am. But I don't. I listen instead.

"Had to help a friend," he says.

"Right. Help a friend open a few bottles possibly?" She might be smiling when she says this, though.

"Mmmm ... possibly?"

I can hear her little laugh and, again, "Right" as I get moving toward the exit and hope they don't hear me.

ROSIE EXPLAINS

I corner her in the cafeteria on Tuesday at lunch, and I don't even care who's watching and what they might say.

She's on her way to sit with a couple of girls from our class, Leah and Marie-Ange. They're what Blair would call "artsy," knitted slouchy hats and headphones dangling around their necks and tunic things over leggings, although Leah wears a graphic T that says *I AM SILENTLY CORRECTING YOUR GRAMMAR*, which I actually think is cool. Blair would not be caught dead wearing something like that, of course. She's all about the skinny jeans and team logos.

"Hey."

Rosie didn't see me coming, but the other two did, and if they were cats, their ears would be standing straight up, tails flicking.

"Hi, Griffin," says Leah, and I try not to glance at the words on her chest as I nod hello.

123

At first, Rosie doesn't even turn around. She just dumps her books and big shoulder bag on the table, as if she hasn't heard me. But of course, she did hear me, and the two other girls are watching the action as if it's a movie, so eventually she has to say something.

"Hi." She turns around then and looks at me, and there's a lot going on there on her face that I can't decipher.

Maybe *Go away.* Maybe *Oh, God, you're such a pain.* Maybe *Don't embarrass me like this.*

Maybe *Okay, let's talk. But not in front of my friends.*

I decide to go with that one.

"Hey, just wondering if we can sit down somewhere and talk about that thing." *What thing, Griffin?* "You know? That thing? The seniors home and the radio station thing?"

"Oh, what Mr. Dunbar was talking about?" Leah asks helpfully.

Of course, that's not what we need to talk about, but Rosie knows this is going to end badly unless she just goes with it, so she does.

And I guess I should feel bad about pushing her, but I can't get the kid's scared face out of my head. So, yeah, I'm doing this for Noah.

"Right, okay." She picks up her stuff and jerks her chin toward an empty table a few rows over, with no one near. "Come on."

124

She's already on the move, so I smile at the two girls—who are loving this scene for all its unspoken drama, I can tell—and follow her. A glance over their heads at my usual hangout table shows Brad, Murph, and Mike glancing our way, too. Me and Rosie. Oh, why not just put on a show and give people something to talk about, right?

"Okay, what?" she says as I dump my pack on a chair and sit down across from her. She doesn't look at me as she speaks. Hands unzipping her shoulder bag, rummaging inside, and finally bringing out a notebook and pen. Smart. She's making it look as if we're actually going to do some work.

"Hey, I don't know why you're mad at me, but I just wanted to talk, that's all," I say, pulling out my computer and opening it up. There: now we look like we're talking shop, not waging some war I don't understand.

And I guess that sinks in, because she lets out a long breath and her shoulders drop an inch or two. And she actually looks at me, although not quite smiling.

"Sorry," she says without moving her lips.

I'll take it. I have no idea what's going on with this girl, but I feel as if I might just be making progress.

"No problem. I was just wondering about the other night, that's all. I mean, I was kind of worried about the little guy, he was so upset." She looks down, bites her lip. "You said you'd explain on

125

Tuesday morning and, you know, here we are, a week later."

She opens her notebook and draws a doodle, but I can tell this is just a regroup tactic, not a stall. A big sigh.

"It's—it's not a big deal," she says finally, so quietly that I have to pull my chair a bit closer and lean in over my computer to hear her.

"It was a big deal to Noah. He was really upset. I mean, he showed up ..."

"Noah gets upset easily," she says before I can go on. She sighs again and looks right at me. "He's a very emotional kid. You've probably noticed."

"Yeah." *Emotional kid.* Okay, that's one way of describing it.

"That first day of school? When we met in the office? Remember?" She glances up and I nod. "I was setting up a sort of plan with Mrs. McRae, for me and Noah. He had a rough first day of school and I had to leave and take him home because our mom was at work. I have to be there for him. He depends on me."

"Okay."

"There's no one else."

No dad? I guess that's what she means.

She writes something in her notebook. No, actually, she's just doodling. Loops, lines, joining, intersecting, circling. I look at it and realize if I tried that it would look like crap, but she's making art. It takes form, a sort of collection of leaf shapes, maybe. Like they're being blown around in the wind.

You're overthinking this, Griff.

"Okay. Here it is," she says, not looking up.

I watch her as she talks. It's not hard to see that this is difficult for her, and yes, I'm starting to feel a bit guilty, actually.

"Noah is not on the spectrum, okay? Mom had him tested and he's not. He's just really, really sensitive about things."

She stops talking. Still doodling, though.

"Okay. He's sensitive about things," I repeat her words, but she doesn't look up or keep talking. Drawing, drawing lines, connecting shapes. I watch and wait. Nothing. "And he gets upset easily."

She sighs and puts her pen down. This time she looks up at me. Her eyes are the most amazing hazel, flecks of yellow mixed in with brown and green.

"He gets upset easily and he gets scared easily. It's just the way he's built. And since our dad died, he only knows a house with me and Mom. And my mom, well, she's ..." And then she stops, as if a door just closed. A beat, and then she keeps going. "And when Mom isn't there, or I'm not there, he's ... I don't know ..." She looks away from me for a moment, across the cafeteria, but not looking at anything, really. Seeing her fatherless home, maybe. "He's scared. Like he thinks he's going to be totally alone or abandoned, I guess." She looks back at me. (*Man, those eyes ...*) "So, the fact that he likes you, actually walks down the street to play hockey with you, this is really big." Pause in which she lifts one eyebrow. "And also, kind of unexpected and weird. Sorry, but it is."

Okay, that makes me laugh.

"Yeah, okay. But the other night, he said you told him to come to my house if he got scared." Eyes drop back down to the page; she picks up her pen. Back in action. Clearly, she doesn't want to talk about this. But all I can see is this little kid in panic mode at my door. "I mean, did you think he might be scared about something? He said some guy was visiting your mom ..."

"Yeah." Short, sharp, and quick glance at me, then down. "Yeah, sometimes my mom uses bad judgment."

I wait. Nothing but the pen on paper. This has got to be the most elaborate and, honestly, beautiful piece of doodle art I've ever seen. This girl has a gift.

"So, that night, there was some bad judgment going on?"

"Yes. That night there was some bad judgment going on." Pen stops. "And I wasn't there, and I should have been. That was bad judgment, too."

Ah.

I wonder what "bad judgment" means to Rosie. Was she out with some guy doing crazy stuff I don't want to even think about? Out with the girls, same?

"I was at the Avonlea," she says in a voice I've heard from

my sisters. The *Get your mind out of the gutter, Griff* voice. "It was for this thing I'm working on, for community service, and I told them I couldn't go out in the evenings, but that was the only time the person from the museum could come, so I had to go. I should have brought him with me, but Mom was home, and they were just talking in the kitchen, and Noah was in his room, and I thought it would be okay. But of course, it wasn't."

"But you told Noah ..."

"Yes." She looks at me as if she's talking to someone who doesn't speak the language. "Yes, Griffin. I told him I'd be home soon but if he was worried, he should go to our neighbor's, but I don't really like her because she's a bit of a gossip, so I told him it would also be okay to go to your house. And, of course, he liked that better. I'm sorry, okay? I'm sorry. I should have checked with you first. I know ..."

Ah. The lightbulb goes on in my head.

"Hey, it was fine, really," I interrupt her before she grinds herself into some pit of guilt. "I was just surprised. And worried about him. But it was fine, really. I was happy to help out. He's a neat kid."

She's watching me as I talk, and I have the feeling she's going through a checklist: *Telling the truth, check. Can be trusted, check. Doesn't think I'm a loser, check. Actually likes my little brother, check.*

"He is neat," she says, and smiles, finally.

"You know, he told me about wanting to play hockey, and how your mom just can't do it." She doesn't say anything, so I carry on. "I was just thinking, maybe there's something I could do to help. Like find some used equipment. There's programs that help with registration fees. I thought if Noah was really keen, and your mom was interested, I could maybe help somehow."

I wind down because she's clearly not buying in. She's actually shaking her head.

"You jocks. Not all problems in the world can be solved by playing hockey, you know," she says.

"What? They can't?" I'm trying to make her laugh, but she doesn't so I change direction. "Hey, I know that. This isn't about pushing hockey on you, or your mom, or anyone. It's about Noah. You can just see, he loves it. It's about what he wants."

"Noah doesn't know what he wants." Her voice drops and her pen has stopped moving. "Scrap that. Yes, he does know what he wants. He wants Mom to be happy. And getting involved in the whole hockey scene or baseball or soccer, or whatever, that we can't afford or fit into her stupid work schedule isn't going to make Mom happy, so your idea is nice, and kind, and generous, but no thanks. We don't need that kind of help."

Wow. I recognize a fierce older sister, something I know all about, having a couple of those myself. Although I don't remember many occasions when they had to be that fierce on my account. Okay, maybe that one time, when I came home from the hospital, and Bella offered to drive six hours to Owen Sound to find that defenseman and beat him up.

I hold up my hands in surrender. "Okay, okay. Forget I mentioned it."

It's tense, and I can tell she's kind of sorry she snapped like that.

Awkward moment means it's time to go. I close my computer and start packing up.

And then she says: "Sorry. And thanks. For Noah, I mean. He really likes doing the ball hockey thing with you."

She's not looking at me as she says it because the pen is back on the paper again, in motion.

"I like it, too," I say. She still doesn't look up, but she nods. I see the hint of a half-smile as I pick up my pack and go.

Truce.

HALLWAY HISTORY

"What's with you and Rosie Courville, Turdiff?"

Yes, Brad is being loud and ignorant in the change room after gym.

Having a last name like Tardiff is a liability around assholes, for sure, and he's definitely not the first one to go this route. But guys I've played against since house league got there before him, so it makes him easy to ignore. Lots of practice.

The part about Rosie, though ...

I'm stuffing my sweaty shirt and shorts into my gym bag, ignoring the pain in my arm, and trying to ignore Brad, too. But that's not the way these things work.

Murph picks it up.

"She's just weird, man."

Most of the guys are already talking, so not many notice this exchange, and I'm pretty sure if they're going to talk about girls, it's not going to be Rosie Courville. Murph and Brad are just doing their thing, trying to include me in their aren't-we-cool, aren't-we-funny way. I'd be happy if they'd leave me out.

Hey, she's an artist. She has a stressful family situation. There's a lot going on there, and you guys shouldn't be such dicks. And by the way, I already have an awesome, smart, and hot girlfriend, so there's no me and Rosie.

That's what I should say but I don't, because what's the point when you're up against a bunch of jerks? I give them a quick not listening glance, just finish packing up and leave the change room.

I don't realize Mike is right behind me until I'm halfway down the corridor.

"Don't mind them. They don't know any better," he says, and I glance over my shoulder.

"Yeah, I know."

He catches up and we walk down the hallway together, dodging oncoming traffic the way you have to between classes.

"Brad's not always such a jerk. His two older brothers are way worse."

That makes me laugh. The idea of Brad being out-jerked by older versions of himself is faintly amusing.

"And, hey, Rosie's cool," Mike says. "We've been in the same class since about kindergarten."

I don't really want to get into a conversation like this. I mean, does he like her? Does he think I'm into her? I glance at him and he just looks like his normal unfazed and large self, walking along while people get out of his way, so I don't think so.

And do I even care? No. But I like that he sticks up for her.

"So, you must have known her when her dad died?"

"Yeah," he shakes his head, remembering. "A couple of years ago. That was really, really tough. Car accident, coming back from Ottawa in a snowstorm and spun out in front of a transport truck."

I saw a YouTube video once, dash-cam footage of a car spinning out on the 401 and slamming into the side of a jackknifed tractor-trailer, so I can just picture it. Huge truck swerving and tilting through a screen of snow. Flashing lights. Ambulance. And then I could imagine the scene you hope you only see on some TV show: OPP showing up at the front door. *We're sorry, but ...*

"Her little brother was just in kindergarten. Yeah, it was bad," Mike says. "So, you know, don't listen to those guys."

"Don't worry. I'm not."

His locker is further down but he hangs out for a minute.

"Hey, Thanksgiving this weekend. You around?"

"Yes, I am, along with multiple members of my family, which means it's going to be loud and messy," I say. Two parents. One sister, solo. One sister, husband and toddler. Aunt and uncle with three kids under age eight. Old uncle, funny, larger-than-life, who tends to drink too much and needs managing.

It must show on my face because Mike laughs and pulls out his phone.

"I'll text you." I glance at him and he shrugs. "In case you need rescuing. We can play NHL 14 in my rec room. Eat turkey leftovers."

Sounds good. Sounds great, actually. We exchange numbers.

"Thanks," I say as he starts to move off. "And hey, thanks for filling me in. About, you know ..."

He nods. "No problem. They're jerks, but they'll grow up one day."

Yeah, jerks do grow up. For a second, I'm back in the hallway at The Legend, eavesdropping on that conversation between Elise and Guy. *They grow up to be adult jerks.*

But I don't say that out loud.

MEDIA GIG, FOR REAL

A couple of weeks later, on a Tuesday afternoon, the boys have their first home game at the arena, and I'm let out of class early to cover it, which is definitely one of the perks of being The Legend 99.1's Youth Intern (official title). *It's not skipping school; it's schoolwork, for that community service course requirement I need, right?* It didn't take much to get permission from the front office. A note from my mom. A call from Guy Martin didn't hurt.

So, now I'm at the arena with computer open on my lap, sitting up in the stands because, for me, that media bench is just too far away from the action.

I want to be close to it all. Ice has a smell, I swear it does. And there's something about the sound of blades that just shoots through me. And everything else—guys calling for passes, the grunts as bodies make contact with boards, ice, and each other at high speed.

For instance, I want to see that Casselman Crusader's face when Mike takes him into the boards. Yeah, Casselman No. 17 is pissed as he tries to get back up onto his skates to rejoin the action. And Mike's face, impassive, already skating away, following the play back up the ice. (I ignore the sympathy pains in my upper arm and shoulder. My imagination, right? Not a flashback, right?) No, it's great. You wouldn't see their eyes—prey and predator—from the official media bench up near the roof. I'm at home here.

"Hey, Griff. Thought I'd find you here in the stands. Taking notes for your report?"

Guy Martin jumps down from the row above and sits down on the bench beside me, The Legend 99.1 jacket supplemented by an expensive scarf and leather gloves. Graying hair combed back and looking pretty GQ. Off duty. Or maybe headed out on a date, I don't know.

"Hey, yeah. Prefer this to sitting up there." I nod up toward the bench. "Too far away from the action."

"For sure. How are the boys doing? No score yet?"

We sit there watching and, of course, we start to analyze the play and players like a couple of TSN commentators. Hey, I *am* on the job, after all, so it's good.

"Mike knows his way around a rink," Guy says. "Brad Scott was drafted by the Junior C team over in Kemptville. Opted out to stay here in varsity for one more year."

Mike is clearly a top-prospect defenseman—skating, puck control, anticipation. Brad is like a truck, barreling through everyone, so strong on his skates and—much to my surprise— really smart with the puck, too. He's a bit of a troublemaker out there, though. Gets away with stuff, messes around with sticks, skates, a little elbow when the refs aren't watching.

"That Casselman No. 29 is one to watch," Guy says, and I zero in on a short but beefy winger, who flies down the right wing with the puck, carves a path inside our defense, and gets a zinger on goal—blocked by Murph, but leaving a huge rebound and a scramble in front of the net.

"Whoa, yeah. Fast, eh?"

"Impossible to stop. Impossible to hit, too."

It feels great to be sitting here with someone who gets it, talking hockey.

I make notes—"Mike creamed 17 into the boards" and "Murph putting on a show in goal" and "Oswald quarterbacking the power play like a pro"—and have a pretty good idea of how the report's going to go, as the game winds down in the third with Glenavon leading 5-1 and playing keep-away for the last few minutes.

At the buzzer, even before the fans have reached full celebration pitch, Guy stands up. "Ready? Let's go."

Scrum time. I follow him down the stairs and past the noisy Hawks fans—most of the school seems to be here now, the female population being quite well represented, as well as quite a few parents—and around the rink to the hallway leading to the dressing rooms.

The Casselman players clomp off the ice and hold us up as they cross the hallway to their room.

"I don't need to get quotes from them, do I?" I ask, and then wish I hadn't.

"Oh, sure, good idea. I'll get Marcel for you. The coach."

Crap, I was hoping I wouldn't have to talk to someone who has just lost a game badly, but there's Guy walking over to the coach as he comes off the ice, speaking to him and pointing at me. The guy shrugs and they come over.

"Marcel Proudfoot. Griffin Tardiff. Go, Griff."

He's a young guy, probably the Phys Ed teacher, and he looks pretty pissed. Not at me, I don't think. Probably pissed at his team for losing 5-1. He stands there, holding a clipboard and looking at me.

"Griffin. Hi." We shake hands. "What do you need?"

"Just a quote for my report, if you don't mind."

"Sure. No problem."

So, I push the voice memo button on my phone and start in, feeling like a complete rookie, which I am, of course.

"So, Coach, just wondering what you think the team needs to work on after that game."

He starts talking about how it's still very early in the season, but they need to tighten up the D, give their goaltender more support, take fewer penalties. I nod and look as if I'm paying attention, but actually, I am completely not listening, because I'm trying to come up with the next question.

But it's okay, because his answer is good. Very coach-like. He winds down quickly.

"That enough for you?" He's already turning away.

"Thanks, that's great," I say, and with a nod to Guy, he stalks off to the dressing room, where I'm pretty sure his players are about to get a lecture on how they need to tighten up their D and give their goalie more support and take fewer penalties.

We head toward the noisy Hawks dressing room where the guys are celebrating.

Mr. Somerville, the Math teacher and assistant coach, is at the door. He nods at Guy and says something with a laugh about waiting for the "press availability," but Guy just laughs back at him and walks into the room, so I follow.

"Media's here," a sweaty, jersey-less Brad yells when I follow Guy through the door, and it gets crazy for a while as they harass me for interviews. Yes, they all think they were the first star of the game.

"Get Brad," Guy suggests, just quietly enough that no one hears. "Assistant captain, first home game, scored a goal. I know he can be a bit of a dick, but he's one of the leaders. Had a good game."

"Right ... okay." I was thinking of Murph, who had a surprisingly awesome game and only gave up one goal on an impossible deflection, but I go with Guy's suggestion.

Brad's all over it, of course, the clichés flying—"Team gave it 110 percent"—but I just let him roll. Guy grins at me. *Yeah, that's Brad.*

"Come on, you can transcribe interviews and write it up at the station. I'll give you a lift home after."

"Sure, thanks. But I just want to ..." I don't finish, but quickly step over sweaty equipment and dodge a few towels to get to Murph. "Hey, man, just wanted to get your reaction to that goal."

The guys actually quiet down a bit. Well, they quiet down after a few variations of *Whoooaa. Murph. Look who's getting the star treatment.*

Murph is red-faced and sweaty, but he answers the question—"Yeah, it was a deflection and I should have had it, you know? But it just happened so fast. Good move by that guy. It happens. But you know, we won. First game of the season here at home and we won. That's all that matters, right?"

The guys have been listening, and a deafening yell goes up when Murph finishes, and I let the recording run for a second, catching that sound of winning, the sound of a winning team.

Man, this is what I miss.

No time to get all nostalgic, though, because Brad stands up and throws a wrestling hold on me, and the guys all roar again. He's still in sweaty shoulder pads, so it smells as well as hurts, but I don't care.

"Griffin Tardiff, the next Legend!" Brad yells above it all and the guys laugh. Some cheer.

But it's time. I need to get out of here and get to work. A glance toward the door ...

Guy's there, watching me. He nods toward the hallway. *C'mon.*

So, I pick my way through the room, catch Mike's eye, and say "good game," before escaping the craziness to follow Guy down the hallway, past some of the fans and what looks like parents and girlfriends still hanging around, and out to the parking lot where his suv waits.

"Good job in there," he says. "Now the fun part."

WHAT JUST HAPPENED?

The Glenavon Hawks kicked off their season with a big 5-1 win over the Casselman Crusaders on Tuesday evening at the Glenavon Community Arena.

Hawks assistant captain Bradley Scott scored two goals in the lopsided win.

"We came out ready to play today and every single guy gave 110 percent. Yeah, it was the first game and there's still stuff to work on. Like, we lost some guys who moved up, but we've got some strong rookies and we just have to stick with the structure and keep digging."

The Hawks are hoping to dig their way back to the divisional finals this season, something that Casselman has not been able to do for three seasons. Casselman coach Marcel Proudfoot knows exactly what his team needs to do.

"It's the first game, very early in the season, obviously, and

the team has a lot of work to do. A game like that—five goals against—obviously we need to tighten up the D and give our goalie a bit more support. We took too many penalties and that hurt us. Hawks played well and we were outgunned on the five-on-four, but as I said, it's early in the season. We'll just have to get to work."

Hawks goalie Kyle Murphy held off a late charge and was beaten only once, on a deflection by Casselman's top scorer last season, James Abara.

"Yeah, it was a deflection and I should have had it, you know? But it just happened so fast. Good move by that guy. It happens. But you know, we won. First game of the season here at home and we won. That's all that matters, right?"

The Hawks next game is against Lancaster on Tuesday in Lancaster. Reporting for The Legend 99.1, this is Griffin Tardiff.

So, I'm lying on my bed, listening to my own report on the radio and hardly hearing it, because I'm still trying to process what just happened.

No, not the game report at the radio station. That was easy. Guy stood in the little control room with Pete, the tech guy, as I sat at the microphone. He suggested where to insert the audio clips, how to pronounce Abara's name. It was teamwork, all easy.

"Great job, Griff," says Guy as I came out of the booth. "I'll give you a lift home."

That's when things got weird.

"I just have to make one stop on the way to your place," Guy says, as we swing out of the parking lot and head down the highway toward my neighborhood.

"Sure, no problem." I'm eyes down, texting Mom that I'm on my way, hoping she realizes this means she should be heating up whatever's in the oven, and getting out the loaf of bread and the peanut butter and whatever else, because I missed supper and I'm starving.

We turn into my neighborhood and I think, *Okay, I guess we're not making a stop, after all.* But instead of driving down to the end of Stanley Street, where I live, Guy turns into the driveway of a small white bungalow.

I expect him to say, "I'll just be a minute," or something, but what he says is: "Come on. A little business for The Legend and I need your help."

I look at him, ready to ask, "What business? What are we doing?"—but he's already getting out of the car.

I don't like this. My parents have told me more than once that I have good instincts—unlike my crazy sisters, who were known in their teenage years to launch themselves into situations of potential, shall we say, excitement. Maybe even danger. Like protest marches. Strikes.

"You're a watcher," my dad, aka Professor Don Tardiff,

Chair of Media Studies at Algonquin College, once told me—and he meant it as a compliment—"You think, and then you act. It's a good way to be, Griff."

So, I'm a bit wary as I get out of the car and follow Guy to the door. I mean, it's a house on my street, and it's Guy, and it's for the radio station, so—right? It must be okay.

"Come on," says Guy, seeing my hesitation. "It's nothing bad. It's about hockey, and The Legend doing something good in the community. Your idea, remember?"

Yeah, I remember. But we haven't even talked about it ...

And then he's ringing the doorbell, and when the door opens, it's Rosie. This is Rosie's house.

She doesn't say anything right away, but the look on her face says it all: *What the hell are you doing here?*

"Hi, Rose." Guy is all cool and friendly and ignores the vibes coming from her. "Is your mom home?"

"What do you want?" Short, sharp. Rude. She says it to Guy and ignores me completely. I have a feeling I just became invisible.

"Who's there?" Noah, in pajamas, comes around the corner from inside and stands next to her. He sees Guy first and he actually steps back.

"Hey, Noah, how's it going?" Guy says.

Then Noah sees me—"Griffin!"—and his face relaxes into a smile.

I smile back automatically, but my brain is trying to process the fact that Guy knows these kids, and clearly, they know him, too.

And then Mrs. Courville comes around the corner and sees first Guy, then me. Her face—it's like she doesn't know whether to smile hello or not.

"Hi, Judy," says Guy. "Just wanted to talk to you about an idea we had at The Legend to get kids from town a little more involved in the hockey scene." He turns to me, drapes his arm across my shoulders. Suddenly we're teammates. "It was Griff's idea, actually."

The three pairs of Courville eyes turn to me—all that same hazel, all intense—and back to Guy.

No, that's not accurate. Rosie keeps her eyes on me, and when I look back, she shakes her head, just the tiniest shake of disgust, and then she turns and walks away.

"Can we come in, Judy?" Guy asks. "Talk about it?"

I disentangle myself from his bro-like arm around my shoulders.

"No!" yells Rosie from somewhere beyond the front entrance.

Mrs. Courville smiles and glances back toward the voice, then glances at me, embarrassed. Man, she still looks so tired, standing there in what looks like hospital scrubs. Maybe she's a nurse?

"Not a great time, Guy, actually. I'm just about to get Noah off to bed before heading out."

Guy doesn't seem bothered by this, but I'm already stepping away, ready to be out of here. He glances at me—*hey, no bailing*—and tries again.

"Sure, Judy, I understand. Sorry, I should have called first." Ya think? "But think about it, okay? Maybe we could come over some other time and talk about this initiative. What we want to do is share news about the programs available for kids who just want to play sports. Maybe do an interview or two? Noah would make a great poster boy for the campaign." He reaches out to ruffle the kid's hair and Noah lets him, frozen, staring, turned to stone.

I want out of here. This is wrong in so many ways, even though I don't understand the dynamic going on between Guy and this family. But the kid ... the kid is now staring at me.

"I don't know, Guy. Maybe we'll talk about it, but really, I have to go," Mrs. Courville is saying, a weak smile, as if she doesn't want to hurt anyone's feelings.

"Sure, okay. Another time. Think about it, okay?" He looks down at Noah. "You too, *mon gars*, okay? Wouldn't you like to be the kid who shows all the other kids that they can play hockey, too?"

Noah stares at him. Says nothing. I hear Rosie's voice: *Not all problems in the world can be solved by playing hockey, you know.*

"Hey, bud," I say to him and his eyes swivel to me. "Whatever, okay? This thing? Don't worry about it now. You want to come take some shots with me after school tomorrow?"

He nods, a shaky grin.

"See you then. Goodnight." I look up at Mrs. Courville, who still has this weird smile plastered on her face, but now she's looking at me, too. "Goodnight, Mrs. Courville. Sorry if we disturbed you."

Yes, I'm acting like an adult because the adult beside me is acting like—I'm not sure. A pushy adult? A jerk?

"Bye, Griffin!" Noah calls to me as the door closes, and I give him a wave and turn to walk down the porch steps without looking at Guy.

He follows me, though, and he seems completely unrattled about the whole weird scene.

"Okay, so it might take some persuading," he says, putting the suv in gear and zooming a little too quickly out of the driveway.

I don't say anything, because I don't quite know how to tell him that I don't want any part in this persuading. Like, leave me out of your little plan. And what's with taking this idea, that I mentioned briefly, once, and turning it into a "campaign" without talking to me about it? But maybe we'll have that conversation another time, because right now, all I can see is Rosie's face, and I need to figure out what just happened there.

So, now I'm lying on my bed, listening to some country music show that came on The Legend 99.1 after the news. I should be doing homework. I should be FaceTiming Blair, who has texted me about five times in the last hour. I should be telling my parents about this weird thing that happened. But I can't. It feels like I was just in a near accident on the highway, adrenalin still pumping.

Which might explain why I'm lying here on my back, with my hands linked under my head, elbows out, and I don't feel any pain in my arm or shoulder. I haven't been able to do this for months. Weird. It's all just weird.

AWKWARD

Yeah, so it's a bit awkward on Wednesday morning, when Rosie and I arrive at the classroom door from different directions at exactly the same moment.

We both hesitate, and she takes a breath as if she's about to say something, but I get there first.

"Hey, about last night," I say, which is unfortunate, because I don't see Brad coming up behind me.

"Last night? What about last night?" He leans in, like he's eavesdropping on a juicy conversation.

Which sends Rosie into the classroom with a face as closed as a slammed door.

"Don't be such a dick." I turn to him, but he just grins at me because, of course, he's good at being a dick.

It's a crap start to a day that is already not off to a great start, thanks to an odd texting session with Blair first thing this morning, as I sat at the kitchen table, downing a bowl of cereal and checking last night's NHL scores.

You ok? Why didn't you text me last night?

I could tell her I was too busy lying on my bed, trying to figure out what had just happened between Guy and the Courville family at their front door—and obviously beyond, somehow. I mean, the undercurrents were raging just in those few minutes of conversation, and there I was, with no idea what was going on.

But I'm pretty sure Blair doesn't need to hear about that.

Sorry, tons of homework and zoned out

All true.

Sure. Bet you were out partying with your new friends

Not a chance. Covered a hockey game for the radio station. Late when I got home

Long pause. I have time to read some of the NHL game reports online, because I can see my message was read, but no response. I start to think she's pissed and won't reply at all.

"Dad and I are going to be late tonight," Mom says, coming into the kitchen to refill her coffee. She's wearing business casual black pants and long sweater, so I know she must be heading into the college today. Dad's already gone, breezing through the kitchen a half-hour ago, travel mug in one hand, computer bag in the other.

"Good report last night, Griff," he'd said. "Sorry I didn't have a chance to see you when I got home. Late meetings, and you were already in bed."

"Thanks." I lift my eyes from the phone and catch him giving me the parental once-over.

"School going okay?"

"Going good, I think."

"And the radio thing? You're enjoying it?"

"Yeah, it's great." *If you don't factor in my mostly helpful and professional boss who sometimes acts like a jerk.* I don't say that, of course.

"I'd like to hear more about it. Maybe tonight?" He's tired, I realize, and apologetic. I haven't really been paying much attention to my parents for the past week or so, but now I realize that Dad's been at early and late meetings more often than he's been home.

"Yeah, good. You can tell me about the stuff going on at the college, too."

He grins at that. "Oh, yes. Fun and games there. All good, though." He raises his mug and heads for the door. "Carry on. We'll catch up ... maybe tonight?"

And here's Mom, a half-hour later.

"You were awfully quiet when you got home last night. Everything go okay?"

So now both parents have asked me if things are going okay.

Much as I'd like their opinion on Guy dragging me along for his pitch to the Courvilles last night, I know this isn't the time.

"All good." I give her the *stop-worrying-Mom* Griffin smile and she squints at me from the kitchen door before heading for the stairs. Something tells me she's not buying it.

"You have a text." She nods toward the phone on the table and is gone.

Boys have a tournament this weekend. Come and help me cheer them on

Plan to. Tell Givens no homework

Mr. Givens is the History teacher at our school in Ottawa. Notorious for assigning essays on Friday that are due first class the following week, which means the weekend disappears.

You're not going to spend the whole time with Jake, right?

Not a chance

How's your girlfriend?

Well, that came out of nowhere.

I'm texting with her right now

Right answer

Okay, so that was a test, apparently. Maybe that little scene at the mall a few weeks ago wasn't as simple as I thought it was. I almost ask, "How's Evan?" but decide against it.

Another pause, as I try to think of something I can say that isn't dangerous, but she gets to it first.

Big news!! Going to Toronto early December for tournament at York. 20 schools. OFSAA warmup

Cool (Volleyball is a safe subject.)

Coach says university scouts will be there. Staying at hotel. Real road trip!! You're allowed to be jealous

She puts up a bunch of party emojis. Oh, yes, she and the girls are going to make the most of it, I'm sure.

Going to Brockville sometime in November to cover a Hawks game. No hotel. There and back on a big fancy bus

It's something Guy mentioned after taping my report yesterday, as we were on the way to our unexpected stop. It's an away game in Brockville, and we get to travel on the bus—a real coach this time, not a school bus—as media. I was really looking forward to it when he mentioned it, but now I'm not so sure. Me and Guy on a bus with the guys. It could be good, right?

Sounds thrilling

Clearly, Blair doesn't think so.

Time to wrap this up. Mom has offered to drop me at school, and I'm already thinking of the conversation I might or might not have with Rosie before class.

School bus leaving. Gotta go

Pause. Nothing. So I try again:

Miss you

It isn't until I'm in the car that she replies:

Miss you too. Better make it up to me on the weekend

Promise

Okay, we're good. This long-distance relationship thing sucks, but we'll be together next weekend, and we'll get back on track. That's what my head is full of as I walk toward homeroom, not seeing the halls of Glenavon Collegiate. Seeing instead my girlfriend in skinny jeans and a hoodie, and her puffy parka, with her bulky-knit Canada toque accenting those eyes, and that smooth skin. My girlfriend, pressed against me for warmth in the stands as we watch the guys on the ice. And after the game—

And there we are, Rosie and me at the classroom door, and her face is a message I can't read. Maybe *Sorry about last night.* Maybe *You're a dick.* Maybe *There are things I want to tell you.* But she doesn't say anything, so I start:

"Hey, about last night …"

And then Brad shows up and wrecks it.

HOCKEY WITH NOAH

After school, I come straight home and get the net out on the driveway, and within minutes, he comes trotting along the sidewalk, holding his stick like a rifle over his shoulder. Which means the shaft slips around and bounces off his ear a few times, but that doesn't stop him. His face is one big smile when he sees me.

"Hi, Griffin! I'm here!"

"Hey, Noah. Thanks for coming." I take a quick wrister at the net and let the ball roll back onto my stick. "No fun doing this alone. Ready?"

The stick falls off his shoulder and bangs on to the asphalt with a crack, and he quickly picks it up.

"Ready!"

For about five minutes, we just scrimmage. Shots. Passes. Me trying to take the ball off him and pretending to get frustrated, which makes him laugh. The kid has a great belly laugh.

"Aw, man. You've got hands like Connor McDavid," I tell him.

He gets by me and takes a high shot that misses the net wide and pings off the white garage door, leaving a mark. That stops him. He looks over at me.

"No problem." I laugh. "You should see the garage door at our house in Ottawa. Polka dots. Thanks to me and Jake missing the net."

"Jake is nice," he says.

"He's my best friend."

Noah stands there, watching me dangle the ball around some spots on the driveway.

"I don't have a best friend right now," he says. "My friend Lucas lived in this house, but he went away when you came."

"He'll be back, don't worry, bud," I say, me still dangling, him still watching the ball. "We just borrowed Lucas's house for this year, while my dad does this thing at the college."

Silence, and I look up at him. He's watching the ball, brows creased. Thinking hard.

"His mom said they were coming back, but I don't know. I don't know if that was for real."

I suddenly remember the dead father scenario. How, in a little kid's world, people sometimes go away and don't come back.

I stop the ball and he looks up at me.

"Lucas is coming back," I say. "Promise. Now get that stick ready because I'm going right through you."

We go one-on-one a bit more, and I'm impressed once again with how good the kid is with his hands on the stick. Can he dangle? No. Can he lift a wrist shot? Yes, and that's not easy when your stick is way too long.

"Nice one!" I tell him, as he roofs another one and I take the ball back on my stick.

"Lucas told me about you coming to stay in this house," Noah says. "His mom knew all about you."

"Yeah, Lucas's mom and my dad are both college teachers, and they're doing a sort of exchange thing this year." He nods, even though I can tell he doesn't quite understand the details. "So, I hope Lucas doesn't mind if we put a few marks on his garage door."

"Lucas plays hockey, so he's probably shooting at your garage door, too!" Noah laughs again.

"Oh, Lucas is a hockey player, eh?" I wonder if this might be a good time to see how the conversation at his front door last night went down, although I think I have a pretty good idea of what might have been said after the door closed on Guy and me.

"Yup. He plays for the Junior Moose." Junior Moose being the name of every minor league team in the Glenavon system, U12 to U18 and beyond. "He tried to get me to play, but I don't want to 'cause Mom said no hockey."

He takes the ball off my stick and passes it to himself, back and forth, forehand, backhand, trying to dangle. His tongue sticks out between his teeth as he gets lost in concentration. I just stay quiet and watch. *'Cause Mom said no hockey ...*

It's going pretty good, until he misjudges and the ball rolls away. I scoop it up with my stick.

"Good job, bud. You're getting it."

"Lucas's mom told me you were a hockey player," he says then. "That's how I knew. When I came to your house that first day. She said you were a star hockey player in Ottawa."

That makes me laugh. "Yeah ... no. Not a star. Is that how you knew my name? That first day?"

"Yeah," he nods. "Lucas's mom told us your name." He reaches for the ball off my stick and starts his dangle practice again. "And then Rosie googled you."

Wait. What?

"Rosie googled me?"

He just keeps passing the ball back and forth, forehand, backhand, eyes on the ball. "Yeah, she googled you. She told me you won some award. And you got hurt in a game."

He looks up at me. "What?" And when he sees me standing there, staring at him, as I try to process what he just said, he gets nervous. "Was that bad?"

"Of course not," I reassure him and scoop the ball away so

quickly that he yells, "Hey!" and follows me back up the driveway toward the net. The next few minutes are all about scrimmaging and adding a few new marks to Lucas's garage door.

The kid is laughing and yelling and having a great time. He's moved on, but I'm still stuck on his words. *Rosie googled you.*

Is that bad? No. Weird, maybe.

"Noah, time for supper."

The two of us turn and see her at the end of the driveway. That drapey green sweater over jeans and various layers, and her arms wrapped around herself, as if she's trying to keep warm, probably. Giving the impression she's holding herself together, more like.

"Aw, I'm not hungry!"

"Noah, come on."

"Hey, bud. It's okay," I scoop the ball into the net so that it stays there. "I'm hungry, too. And I have homework."

"Aw." He's disappointed, maybe because we were having such a fascinating conversation, but he only smacks his stick on the driveway once and then trails it behind him toward his sister and the walk home.

I look up at her and, at first, she won't make eye contact with me. Instead, she smiles at her brother, squeezing his shoulder. "You've got the moves, kid," she says, and that makes him laugh.

Then she looks up at me and there's this moment, when I

swear I can hear her say, *Let's just not talk about it, okay?* Last night, she means. So I nod.

And then she says: "Listen, I wanted to ask you about this project I'm doing at the Avonlea sometime. Elise Rogers has been talking to my supervisor, Mrs. McAndrews, and it involves the museum, and the radio station, and recording some stuff, and since you're there at The Legend already, I just thought ..." She winds down, shrugs.

What I really want to ask her is, *Why don't you get someone who really works at The Legend 99.1 to help? Why are you asking me, the sports intern?*

But I don't, because I'm pretty sure this has something to do with avoiding Guy Martin.

"Sure. Let's talk about it tomorrow. You can fill me in."

"I'll let Mrs. McAndrews know. She'll probably get Mrs. Rogers to contact you." She nods and turns to go, one arm around Noah's shoulders.

"Bye, Griffin!" Noah calls to me, as they head back down the sidewalk toward their house, and I give him the nod.

"Bye, Noah. Nice stick work today."

He grins and waves, then turns back to his sister. I hear him say, "I told him you googled him," and she leans over and says something to him that I can't hear, but she doesn't look back at me.

THE LEGEND

"Did you see the game last night?" Brad is at my locker next morning, before I've even got my jacket off.

"The game" could mean anything, but I'm pretty sure I know the one he's talking about.

Flames and Stars. The game where our local Ottawa boy Nathan McCormick of the Calgary Flames had a run-in with the boards late in the second period and missed the third.

"Brutal."

Yeah, I was watching, and it made me feel sick for a minute, because it was exactly the same play that got me here, months later, still waking up at night with the pain of a shattered bone. Oh, yes, and watching from the sidelines.

"All they're saying is upper-body injury." Brad leans on the locker next to me, shaking his head. "Sucks, man. I hope he's okay for the Sens game next weekend."

I do, too, but not just for Nathan McCormick's sake.

Email last night from Guy:

Interested in coming with me to the Canadian Tire Centre this weekend when the Flames are in town? Accreditation for both of us to watch the game from the press box. I'm covering Nathan McCormick's return to Ottawa for The Legend and you can see how a major media event happens.

If you're available and interested, let me know so we can arrange accreditation for you.

I respond right away. Are you kidding?

And then I remember Blair. The guys' tournament. Making it up to her and all that. Shit.

I'll just have to figure it out, because no way I'm going to miss this opportunity. I mean, the chance to go behind the scenes at an NHL hockey game, get up close to the players, the coach. The *scrum*. A real scrum. Of course, I'm not going to ask any questions, but just to be standing there, with all those other reporters, phone out to record it all. Maybe Josh Drouin will be there and Guy can introduce me ...

Dream come true.

Brad is still talking and I zone back in. Something about the play where McCormick got nailed, and no penalty.

"They'll nail him next time they play the Flames, for sure. And the refs, what a joke. That was a dirty hit for sure."

I don't say anything, because I'm an expert in how quickly these violent situations develop along the boards, how sometimes it's just physics: mass, momentum, damage done.

Murph and Mike come by as I slam my locker shut, and it's hockey talk all the way down to our classroom.

"Game Tuesday in Embrun," Mike says to me. "You coming?"

"No, Guy's looking after this one."

"Yeah, he's the regular reporter for all the teams. Us, the Moose. Too bad."

"I'll be going to the Brockville game in a few weeks, though. Guy got us both on the team bus for that one."

"Sounds good. That'll be a good game."

I wonder if it's okay to tell him about Ottawa and decide it probably is, especially since Brad and Murph are ahead of us now, loudly dissecting the McCormick non-call and injury, and paying no attention to us walking behind. The last thing I need is Bradley Scott, The Human Loudspeaker, blasting my news all over school. But Mike, he's different.

"Hey, get this." I go for it. "I just found out I'm going to get accreditation to watch the Sens-Flames game with Guy this weekend. From the press box at the Canadian Tire Centre." I hope I don't sound too much like a kid at Christmas. "Guy's hoping for an interview with McCormick, so hopefully he's okay by then."

"That's awesome!" Mike is genuinely impressed. "So cool. Maybe you'll see Josh Drouin up there." He gives me an elbow. "The Legend meets The Legend."

I laugh that one off, and don't mention that the same thought had already crossed my mind.

EMAIL FROM ELISE

I'm deep into my math homework when the message comes in. And at first, I ignore it, because there have been way too many distractions tonight.

Like texts from Blair being all apologetic about yesterday's cranky exchange, and a whole lot of other stuff flying back and forth that I'm not going to share with anyone, and will probably delete from my phone before the night's out, just in case my mother ever gets hold of it.

Texts with Jake—uncomplicated arrangements for coming to stay at his house this weekend, and lots of crazy all-caps about the Sens-Flames gig in the press box.

Text from Mom, saying they're delayed at their evening dinner meeting and I should go wild with the Kraft dinner, or order in from the pizza place in town. "Also, eggs," she says, because she knows I love breakfast for dinner.

All this between checking scores and trying not to drift into dreamland, picturing myself at the Canadian Tire Centre with my accreditation around my neck, hanging out in the media zone up in the rafters, while the game unfolds down there on the ice. Holding a coffee cup and my phone and coolly chatting with Josh Drouin, or the CBC crew, or running into Nathan McCormick in the hallway outside the press box, if he's still injured and watching the game from up there with some of the guys ...

Oh, and back in reality, doing my math homework: *Integral of sin (2x) from 0 to pi/2...*

Another buzz on my phone, and my head is so full of other stuff that I almost ignore it. But then I tell myself I'm so distracted already, I might as well look.

An email from Elise Rogers:

Hi Griffin,

We're all set for the game October 17 between the Senators and Flames. You can pick up your accreditation at the Media entrance of the Canadian Tire Centre (Gate 3, upstairs). You can travel with Guy to and from the game, or you can arrange your own transportation. If you're traveling with Guy, I'd like to have a letter of permission from your parents, please. Just let me know.

There's another project, not sports related, that I wonder if you'd be interested in helping us with.

The Avonlea Seniors Lodge is doing a special "Memory" project as part of a partnership exhibit, involving The Legend 99.1, Glenavon Collegiate, and the Dunvegan Museum. It will feature three of Avonlea's residents in a multi-media presentation: recorded stories of "life in our town," as well as portraits of the speakers, drawn by the Lodge's student intern, Rose Courville (you might know Rose from GCI—she's a very talented young artist).

Your role would be to record the audio while Rose interviews and draws the residents. We will supply the recording equipment, and Pete will help you edit and produce the final audio files here at the station.

If you're interested, please reply to this email and we'll set up a time to organize the project with Avonlea's administrator Elizabeth McAndrew, and with Rose.

No worries if this is not something you're interested in. I know Guy is keeping you busy with hockey coverage, and of course you have school obligations, too. Guy or Pete can take over the recording side of this project if you're not available.

Thanks, Griffin. You're doing a great job for The Legend 99.1.

Best,

Elise

I read it twice, just to make sure of the details—especially that part about picking up my accreditation at Gate 3 of the Canadian Tire Centre, and the line about Rose being a talented young artist—and then I email Elise back.

Because, yeah, I'm in.

SNOW

The pain wakes me up and I lie there for a while, just breathing, until the throbbing turns into nerves easing out of panic mode. Slowly turns into a dull ache. Then I finally open my eyes.

It's dark. Of course it's dark. It's 3:36 AM, but there's something happening around the edges of the window, so I get up and cross over to my desk, push the blind aside.

Snow. Not the light mini-blasts we've had so far this fall, the kind that just appears overnight and means you walk through the ridges and drifts to school, wearing your hiking boots, and then it melts off and you're stuck slogging home in boots and wishing you were wearing running shoes. No, this is the real snow. Ottawa Valley snow. The one that blows in, settles deep and heavy, and requires the search for shovels stowed in the garage, because it's probably sticking around until April.

The wind is up, too, so outside it's a screen of huge white

flakes working their way earthward at an angle, backlit by the streetlights. The trees are covered. Roofs. Any cars left in driveways look like giant scoops of ice cream.

Driveways. I peer down to the right. Ours is a solid plain of snow. Deep snow and getting deeper.

And what flashes across my middle-of-the-night brain?

Noah. Taking shots on the driveway. Until I get it cleared, our little after-school dangle-fests are on hold.

Tomorrow. I cross the room, crawl back under the covers and roost. Close my eyes. I see the kid and his big stick, flicking the ball up into the corner of the net, and turning to me with that wide-eyed grin. *I did it! Hey, Griff! Did you see?*

The wind howls a little and I burrow, drift off. My arm doesn't hurt anymore.

OTTAWA WEEKEND, PART 1

"Come *on*, Griffin. If I have to listen to one more word about how fabulous it's going to be tomorrow night at the frigging Canadian Tire Centre, I'm going home."

It's Friday night, and we're huddled close together in the last row of the stands at the Rockway Community Arena, which has to be one of the coldest arenas in the city—probably the reason the school board chose it for the tournament. Two decent rinks, but dingy dressing rooms, crappy concession stand, and heaters that don't always work. Probably doesn't cost much to rent.

The huddling part is great, or at least it would be if Blair would show just the slightest interest in my upcoming media adventure this weekend.

Yes, okay, it's just possible I'm being a jerk.

But I can't get away from it, the anticipation, the crazy scenes that keep popping up in my head. Me and Guy in the actual press box, sharing the space with professional reporters and media people, cameras and computers.

Okay, it is true that The Legend 99.1 has reporters and announcers and cameras and computers, and all sorts of cool recording equipment that I'm kind of getting familiar with, thanks to tutorials from Guy and Pete, the main tech guy. But come on, a real press box at a real NHL arena? How can she not get this?

"Sorry," I say into her ear and squeeze her hand, which is tucked into my jacket pocket.

She turns her head so our eyes are inches apart, noses touching.

"I forgive you because you're so cute." Kisses me. "You and your big Hockey Night in Canada fanboy dreams. But can we please just watch the game? Cheer on the guys?" She kisses me again, longer this time, pulls back to whisper: "Or maybe not?"

An airhorn blast makes us jump, ending that particular romantic moment. But it's okay, because we now see the boys down on the ice, celebrating a goal—Evan's, judging from the way he's leading the glove-tapping down the bench—and suddenly the game is tied with under two minutes left in the third.

"We should pay attention," says Blair. Turns her head and burrows into my neck for just a moment.

"I guess." She's very good at this. We smile at each other and turn back to the game.

I'm actually starting to think that the game isn't all that important. I've got my girlfriend here beside me—my girlfriend who's in a really good mood—and I've got the Canadian Tire Centre waiting for me tomorrow night, so maybe it doesn't matter that I'm not out there on the ice, where I should be ...

... on a line with Jake, wheeling down the right wing, waiting for his pass, just like No. 28, that new guy, is doing right now. Jake and No. 28, and Serge back on the point, keeping the puck in. A cross-ice pass to No. 28, then back to Jake, who's winding up, skate save—rebound—No. 28 fires it five-hole and there's that freaking airhorn again.

I'm standing now, Blair beside me, and she's yelling and clapping with everybody else. I watch Jake and No. 28 celebrate with a huge hug that spins them both around, then the guys rush in, and they move to the bench so No. 28 can lead another celebratory tap down the line of outstretched gloves, and it's so loud.

"You've got this!" Blair yells down toward the ice, where nobody can hear her in the crowd noise, but that doesn't stop her. "Come on, Jake! Come on, Evan!" She leans down to high-five some fans further along the row below us, some of the girls from school. "Isn't this fantastic?" They're talking now, laughing, and she takes a few steps toward them so they can celebrate together.

And standing there by myself for a second, a split-second,

I feel as if I could just turn and go, fade away, leave this crappy arena and this game behind, and no one would notice. Not Blair, not the guys on the ice, not anyone. Because I should be out there, too, and it's killing me that nobody notices.

Blair's back. She wraps her arm around mine and our hands are once again joined and stuffed in the pocket of my jacket. She presses up beside me and gives a little shiver of excitement.

"This is so awesome! I have a good feeling about this game." She laughs, eyes on the ice as play resumes, and Evan scoops up the puck and leads the rush into the offensive zone. She yells so loud I almost flinch: "Come on, Evan!"

No, she hasn't noticed that all I can see is the place where I should be.

OTTAWA WEEKEND, PART 2

On Saturday morning, Blair and I are back at the arena, watching Jake and the guys get hammered by a team from Nepean, and not talking much.

This is probably because she's pissed at me. She wanted to skip the game and go hang out at the mall, or better yet, her family room, but I said I'd promised Jake I'd be there, and she obviously doesn't consider promises made to Jake as important as opportunities to spend time with her.

"You're part of the team, man," Jake said to me last night, as I lay on the air mattress in his room, trying not to sound too pathetic about my stupid arm and being stuck on the sidelines. "Everybody knows that. We want you there."

Yeah, maybe not No. 28, I think. But I'm glad he said it. It helps.

But it means when Blair texted me this morning about blowing off the game and meeting her somewhere for "just us time," I had to reply that I was already on the way to the arena with Jake and his dad. Pretty hard to change plans at that point.

Texting silence for a good half-hour.

"Blair giving you grief?" Jake asks, as we hang out briefly in the warm concession area, and he sees me checking my phone for the tenth time.

"Yeah. She's not feeling the hockey love this morning, I guess."

"You don't have to stay, you know. I get it. I know this sucks for you."

"Trying to get rid of me?" I ask. I'm joking, I think.

"No way," he says. "It's just ... I know what Blair can be like. And with you away in Glenavon, it's hard on you guys. So I get it."

I shrug. "Yeah, maybe, but I'm still staying." I check my phone again. Nothing.

"You know ..."

I look up at him and he squints at me. I know Jake well enough to recognize when he has something on his mind. "So, about Blair ..."

He has Blair on his mind?

"Hey, guys."

We turn, distracted by Evan and Marc, our goalie, who have just arrived, hockey bags and goalie pads in tow, parents and

Marc's girlfriend Yvette right behind. The foyer is starting to get crowded and loud. Almost time for the guys to get ready for warm-up.

"Blair not coming today?" Evan asks, looking around.

"Not yet, no." No way Evan needs any explanations about my moody girlfriend.

My phone buzzes and I take a quick look. It's her.

On my way

"All good?" Jake grabs his hockey bag and turns toward the glass doors to the ice surface and the hallway to the crappy dressing rooms.

"Yeah, we're good. Good luck."

And they need it, because this Nepean team is so fast, nobody can stop them. The score is 5-1 (No. 28 the only scorer for our side) and we're not even halfway through the game.

"God, this is awful," says Blair, but she doesn't turn her head, so the words float out into the cold, loud arena on breath we can see. We're close together, but she's keeping her hands in her own pockets today. I'm being punished.

"Yeah, this is a really good team," I try to keep it neutral but I fail, because I don't feel neutral today. I feel crappy.

"Why are we even here?" Blair turns to me with a quick movement that puts a space between us. Her head is tilted a bit, mouth a straight line. She's obviously feeling crappy, too, and the way to feel better is for us to leave the arena, together, and go somewhere, anywhere. I know it would be so easy to make her happy again.

Jake said I don't need to be here. Blair doesn't want to stay. So why am I here?

Because I want to be here, because this is my team. These are my guys. Yes, even annoying Evan, and the unknown super-talented No. 28, who is currently ripping up the right wing where I'm supposed to be. I'd pick a hockey arena with my guys on the ice any day over a mall or, to be honest, Blair's family room when her mom's not home.

"Sorry. Maybe we can go someplace after? It's just that I wanted to be here to support the guys." But I know what's coming, because I can see it in her face.

"Well, Griffin, I hope you and *the guys* enjoy yourselves," she says and stands up. "'Cause I'm out of here."

She's down the arena steps and gone from view, so fast I don't even have time to process it or say anything. Am I supposed to follow her? Yes, probably. I ignore the glances of some girls sitting nearby and stare at the ice, trying to decide whether I should just bail and go after her.

My phone buzzes.

See you at Gate 3 tonight at 6 PM. Dress nice

Guy Martin.

And as I'm reading his message, the crowd erupts again. Nepean now leads 6-1 and their fans are going nuts. I see Jake skate over to the bench, head down. Evan, right behind him, slams the gate so hard that it opens again. So he slams it harder, and Coach Melville comes down the bench and leans over to tell him to stop. Yeah, it's a shit show out there.

I look down at Marc, who's bent over in the crease, staring down as if he wants to break through the ice and disappear. Behind him, on the other side of the glass, Blair rounds the end of the rink and goes out the exit doors. She doesn't even look back.

I text Guy:

Can't wait

PRE-GAME

"Text me after," says Jake as we walk from the parking lot to the arena. He and his dad got tickets for the game, just so they could drive me. "No worries if you have to hang out afterward for a while. You know, interviewing Nathan McCormick and the guys, and asking all the big questions in the scrum, and all that stuff."

"Yeah ... no. I'm just along for the ride on this one." But I can't help grinning because ... well ... I may not be asking the big questions, but I'll still be there.

I feel a bit like I'm the one stepping on the ice, thoughts racing around in that familiar pre-game buzz, the nerves. *Am I ready?*

"Have a great time, Griff. We'll watch for you up in the press box," says Mr. Allen as we get to the doors.

They wave me away and I go in search of Gate 3, which takes a while and several stops to ask staff, but I eventually find it and

Guy, waiting for me, wearing his dark brown The Legend 99.1 leather jacket over shirt and tie.

"Enjoy every minute," Dad had said on the drive to Ottawa Friday afternoon. He had agreed with Guy and told me to step up the wardrobe. No jeans. My one expensive cashmere sweater with dress pants, dress shirt. Tie good but not necessary.

"Really?" A tie? I thought that was just a thing with NHL players. "Isn't the press box a bit more relaxed?"

"Think of this as a job interview, Griff," he had said in total college professor mode.

And, of course, he's right. That's what I'm thinking about as I nod hello to Guy.

A job interview for a career in sports broadcasting. It could happen, right?

He gives me the once-over and nods. Looks like I dressed nice enough. "Ready, kid?"

"I think so."

Pretty sure he can see that I'm pumped up a bit, but he doesn't say anything, just grins and leads the way.

"You're going to have fun," he says. "Come on."

Of course, I try to act cool going through the security check, like this is all familiar territory, trying not to stare as a couple of familiar broadcasters go by and nod at Guy. Yeah, I'm cool, but I'm also taking a million photos and texting them to Jake and my mom. Decide to leave Blair off the list, because she hasn't replied to any of my texts since she walked out the arena doors this morning.

They let me in

A picture of my press pass with its graphic of three Senators players over the words SINGLE-GAME PASS and my name.

Made the list

The assigned seating chart with our places on the press box overlooking the ice. *55—99.1FM Griffin Tardiff* right below *54—99.1FM Guy Martin*. Right there with the radio announcers and reporters and random people from other media outlets and NHL teams.

View from the press box

The TV lights aren't on yet, so the ice reflects the glow from the jumbotron and some of the lighting around the seats. Up in the rafters, the banners—Alfredsson, Phillips, championships from the 1920s—hang in the shadows.

"A bit like being in church, isn't it?" Guy says.

When I look over at him, he's grinning at me, nodding.

"Yeah."

We just stand there behind our assigned places at the smooth, dark gray counter that is the press box table—yup, there we are, numbers 54 and 55—and look out at the huge, slightly humming space in front of us.

"Thank you so much," I say. "This is ..."

"No problem, Griff. And yeah, I know."

THE LEGEND

We're standing in the hallway outside the Visitors dressing room, as directed by the Flames PR guy, waiting for Nathan McCormick to show up for a brief scrum before warm-up starts.

I can't believe I'm actually standing here with Guy and this small group of media people, one of them with a video camera, holding a microphone. I appear to be the best dressed, too, which is a bit embarrassing (*I hear you, Dad! But the tie, why?*) but it doesn't really matter because I'm just on the fringe, keeping out of the way.

Guy is right in there, though. Joking with a guy who I think is from the *Ottawa Citizen* and another reporter, a woman, from the online sports media outlet, *The Athletic*.

"Bigger story than the game, eh?" Guy says to the woman and she laughs.

"The local boy angle is pretty big, you've got to admit."

"He'll be out in a minute." The PR guy, James something, pops up at the door of the dressing room and disappears just as quickly, and there's a brief moment when everyone stops talking, ready for whatever comes next.

That's when someone breezes past me, there on the fringe, and moves up to the camera guy, reaching for the microphone.

"Thanks, Steve. Got a bit delayed upstairs," he says.

Josh Drouin.

Josh Drouin, The Legend, standing two meters away from me.

On TV, you can tell he's a young guy but, in person, he looks like he's still in school—all close-shaved, smooth-skinned, hair scooped up with product. Expensive suit and tie. Totally cool.

"Hey, kid," says Guy, and Josh turns, smiles in recognition, and puts out his hand.

"Guy! Fantastic to see you. How are things at The Legend?"

They chat and Guy looks back at me, ready to pull me up for an introduction, I hope, just as Nathan McCormick shows up in the dressing room doorway with the PR guy.

All eyes, cameras, and phones immediately turn toward him.

McCormick is huge. I had no idea how massive he is. Even in his sleek dark suit and tie, no hockey equipment, he's a presence. His left arm is in a sling and he stands there, looking as if he'd rather be anywhere else than in this hallway with everyone wanting something from him. His expression is all *Go away.*

Josh Drouin gets it started, asking about the injury.

"Yeah, separated shoulder." McCormick stands still, as if the shoulder still hurts, which I bet it does. It's only been a few days. "The doctor says about two or three weeks, depending on how it goes."

More questions from Josh, from one of the other reporters. More answers.

"Yeah, still some pain, but the training staff is managing that."

I've got my phone out now, taking photos because, of course, I have to send this to Jake.

"Nathan, Guy Martin from The Legend 99.1 in Glenavon." I see that McCormick recognizes him, nods. (*That photo on the wall of Guy's office ...*) "Not the trip home you hoped for, I guess, but still good to be back?"

"I could have stayed back in Calgary, yeah, but Rick asked if I wanted to make the trip anyway, and I said yes, because of this stop in Ottawa. And Montreal." He shrugs and immediately grimaces. Shrugging is a bad idea with a separated shoulder, obviously. I wince, too.

"You've got good memories of living and playing in the region?"

It's kind of a loaded question, because, of course, everyone knows about that year he was suspended after that fight at the World Juniors, hiding out at some private boarding school in a town just down the highway from Glenavon. But McCormick doesn't seem to mind.

"Yeah. It's home, really. I have family here. Friends here and in Montreal, and we're there on Monday, so it's nice to be able to connect. Just wish I could help the team, too."

Guy nods and someone else jumps in with a question.

Check this out

I text Jake a photo of Nathan McCormick in the middle of the scrum with all the phones, and the back of Josh Drouin's head with his mic, the light from his video guy splashing all over everything.

And pretty soon the scrum is over. McCormick disappears back into the Flames dressing room and the little herd of reporters drifts away down the hall toward the elevators to the press box.

Jake texts back:

Living the dream

"So, Josh, meet my latest project," says Guy, and I look up from my phone to see Josh Drouin standing right in front of me, smiling. "Griffin Tardiff. Student intern at the Legend 99.1 FM. Sound familiar?"

We shake hands. Yes, I just shook hands with Josh Drouin, who appears on my TV screen practically every time I watch a hockey game.

And yes, I am in full fanboy mode.

"Nice to meet you, Griffin. Great opportunity, isn't it? The Legend? I have such good memories of doing reports on the Moose and the GCI teams."

"He's doing a great job," Guy says. "Might even make it to the big leagues like you one day."

Laying it on a bit thick, but okay.

"Thinking about media as a career?" Josh asks. He seems to have all the time in the world, even with a live broadcast starting in just over an hour.

"Maybe, yeah. It's definitely on my radar."

"And hockey's your game, is it? You play?"

The woman from *The Athletic* comes by, glances at Josh, and then pulls Guy aside to say something to him. Something funny from the looks of it, 'cause he's grinning and laughing a little. Whatever. I'm in conversation with Josh Drouin ...

"I do, yeah. But not this year." He actually looks interested, so I fill him in. "I was injured last year in Ottawa in a high school game. Broke my arm pretty badly, so I'm not back yet."

"Yikes, that's painful. Sorry to hear it." He nods over his shoulder at the Flames dressing room. "You and Nathan, eh? You must know what it's like."

"Yeah. I like that the team brought him along, though, made him feel part of things still, you know?"

Josh is nodding at me. "I know. I like that, too."

Yes, Josh Drouin and I are having a moment.

A moment that's interrupted by Guy laughing loudly, as the woman reporter says something under her breath and walks away toward the elevator, laughing at him over her shoulder.

"Well, I've got to get back to work," says Josh, as Guy wanders back toward us, still grinning. "Great to see you, Guy." They shake hands. "And great to meet you, Griffin. You guys are coming to the coaches scrums, right?"

"Wouldn't miss it," says Guy. "Got to give Griff the full experience."

Josh grins at me. "For sure. See you guys later."

He walks back to his video guy and disappears down the hallway, toward the ice surface or the home dressing room, or whatever his next assignment is for the pre-game.

"There you go," says Guy. "First scrum. Got to meet Josh. What do you say we head up to the press box and watch a hockey game?

PRESS BOX

So much happens during the game that I have trouble processing it all.

I know what a hockey game sounds like, but so high up in this cavern of an NHL arena, with the sound system and the crowd and the guys on the ice, not to mention all the talking going on around me here in the press box—it's like somebody cranked up the volume beyond max.

Add the lights, action all over the white ice, jumbotron flashing—just the avalanche of color and movement in the stands and around me. Yeah, you could say it's a bit over-stimulating.

Of course, I love it.

The hot dogs arrive during the first intermission.

"Am I allowed?" I ask Guy and he just laughs at me.

"Yes, you're allowed. Go for it."

So I do. Actually, I go back for a second one, too.

"Not bad," says the guy next to me at the serving table. His media pass says he's from a radio station in Montreal. "Not nearly as good as ours at the Bell Centre, though."

He says it and then takes an enormous bite, smiles at me while he's chewing, so I guess Ottawa is doing okay. More than okay. A constant supply of pop from the soda fountain, coffee, tea, hot chocolate. Oh, and popcorn. So much popcorn. The media will not be going hungry. It's awesome.

The game, however, isn't awesome. It's a bit of a rout, actually, as the Sens keep lighting it up and Calgary just can't get anything going. A bit like my guys and their tournament, which ended for them after a two-loss day today.

Yes, I was at both games. And no, Blair didn't come back. Or reply to my texts.

I keep checking, though, just in case. She can't stay mad forever, can she?

I haven't been talking much (mostly because I don't want to sound like an amateur around all these professionals) and Guy already has his story on McCormick, so he's just lounging at the media bench beside me, drinking coffee and doing a sort of one-man commentary.

"Terrible pass there. What's he thinking?" The Calgary defense is letting everything through. "They're missing McCormick."

It's starting to bug me, partly because a piece of my brain is stuck on MIA Blair, but also because I just want to soak it all in, enjoy watching the pros—the ones on the ice and the ones all around us, too—but he won't shut up. So, when he stands up near the end of the second period and says, "Got some friends in the stands tonight, Griff, so I'm going to connect with them for a while. I'll be back," it's a bit of a relief.

Then a final question. "You don't need a drive back to Glenavon, do you, Griff?"

"No, I'm good. My buddy's here. I'm staying with him tonight, so I'm meeting up with him later."

"Good, great. See you down at the post-game scrum. You can find your way, right? Just ask anyone," he says, already packing up his iPad, phone, like he's calling it a night. "Follow the crowd." He grins.

"Sure, no problem."

I'm a bit surprised, him leaving the teenage intern here by himself, but whatever. He knows he can trust me not to do anything stupid.

So, I'm alone in the press box, and I can't help myself from doing something stupid. Yes, I take a selfie and send it to Jake and my mom.

Just hanging out in the press box at the Sens game. Yawn

Mom responds immediately with hearts and hand claps and thumbs up. Oh, my mother and the emojis.

Jake is more practical:

I guess you don't want to leave early? Sens got this one

The score is now 5-1 and Ryan has a hat trick. It's a massacre, basically, but there's no way I'm leaving.

Not. A. Chance. Post-game scrum

There's a TV time-out and I lean back and look around at people up and down the bench near me, some of them hunched over, typing. Some on their phones. Some just watching. I look back out at the ice and imagine myself sitting here, writing my game report.

The Calgary Flames rolled into the Canadian Tire Centre in Ottawa on Saturday night, unaware they were about to face a Senators team on fire. Led by Tyler Ryan's hat trick, the Senators ...

And then my phone buzzes.

I figure it's Jake, but no. It's a text from Blair.

You're missing the party

It's from the team party that Jake and I were supposed to be at—until this gig at the Sens game came up and plans changed.

And then a photo comes through. Her, smiling dopily into the camera, with Evan's arm draped around her shoulders, and an equally dopey look on his face, close to hers.

The Sens score again and the horn goes, and it's just so loud I find myself pushing away from the table and heading for the exit, the hallway, somewhere away from the noise.

Away from that text. That photo.

But my phone's in my hand and I can't help glancing at it again, not even aware of which direction I'm going. Blair and Evan and their dopey grins, and I can just hear them—*You're missing a great party, Griff, but if that's what you want, okay. You and Jake have a fun time, whatever*—and I look up to find myself way down the hallway, outside the special rooms, where the team scouts are, and the executives and VIPS.

And apparently, where the players who didn't dress for the game are hanging out, too, because there's Nathan McCormick, leaning on the wall with his phone out, scrolling with his one free hand.

I stop, because it occurs to me, I'm probably not supposed to be here, and he looks up. Maybe he recognizes me from the pre-game scrum, I don't know, but he nods at me. Looks back down at his phone.

There's a sudden blast of sound from the game. Another Sens goal. I'm about to turn around and get out of there, but as I do, I see McCormick take his eyes off his phone and stare into space, listening. His face is like stone.

And I swear, I know exactly what he's thinking and how that feels.

I back away, turn and go, back to the press box, where I stand around, wondering if I should just get Jake and go, skip the post-game scrum.

Guy would notice, though, and as the person who went to the trouble of getting me accreditation, he might not think that's cool, even if he did dump me for his friends in the stands.

So, I wait as the noise level hits jet-taking-off levels and the Sens skate off with a 7-1 crushing of the McCormick-less Flames. And then I follow the rest of the media back down to the hallway outside the Flames dressing room and stand there on the edge, not really present.

Wondering what I should reply to Blair.

POST-GAME

"Hi, Griffin."

"Oh, hi." It's Josh Drouin, pausing in front of me as I lean on the wall, staring at the picture of Blair and Evan. No sign of Guy, and I'm not sure of the protocol.

And of course, I'm not going to be the nerdy nobody who asks the Calgary coach any questions.

Josh is holding his mic, one eye on the dressing room doorway, where only four or five media guys are hanging out.

"Always interesting to hear what the losing coach has to say," he says.

"Yeah, for sure." I'm still inside Blair's text, so I know I must sound and maybe look a bit incoherent. I try to pull myself together. I mean, Josh Drouin has stopped to talk to *me*. I don't want to waste it.

"I guess all the action will be at the Sens room, with the Sens coach?" I ask him and he nods.

"Yeah, but they'll wait 'til I get there." He raises his mic so the sign on it is clearly visible. "Host broadcaster and all that."

Right. The protocols. It must be a bit like dealing with royalty, all these team and broadcast rules.

"Guy not around?"

"He's around somewhere," I shrug and take a look over my shoulder, expecting to see him sauntering down in the hallway. I don't mention that he went to meet up with some friends. Maybe he's partying with them. Something tells me that is a definite possibility.

"Yeah," Josh sighs, grins, nods at me. "Guy." As if he knows exactly what I was thinking. As if maybe I'm not the only one who's heard conversations like the one I overheard in The Legend 99.1's hallway last week, between him and Elise.

There's a stir in the small group, as the Flames coach steps out of the dressing room into the hallway.

"Showtime," says Josh and moves to the front. His video guy has arrived and starts filming. Lights on. Everybody moves in around Josh.

Except for me. I just hang at the back and watch the pros in action.

"Tough game, Rick. What did you say to the players when they came off the ice?"

Josh gets it started, and there's the expected lines about

effort and not following the structure, and the Sens power play and goaltending. You can tell coach Steeves just wants this to be over.

And so do I. It's like my brain is one of those kaleidoscopes, images just flying by, circling, all colors, hard to distinguish.

Blair and Evan—their faces. What is that? Missing the party. The guys on the ice last night, this morning, this afternoon. The ice, so far away and me watching, always watching. Left out. Nathan McCormick in the hallway, looking up at nothing, as the horn sounds for another goal against his team.

Snap out of it, Tardiff. I look up to see if Guy's coming, if this scrum is over, and I can go find Jake and head back to his place and crash.

But I don't see Guy. Instead, I see Josh Drouin looking at me, nodding his head toward the coach. Some guy on the other side of the small group of reporters is asking a question, so Josh is momentarily off mic. He raises his eyebrows at me, nods, and mouths: *Ask something.*

"Me?" I mouth back at him. Not a chance.

"Yes, you." He nods again. *Come here.*

I have no idea what's making me move, but I do. I walk over to Josh and stand beside him.

"Great opportunity," he says to me quietly, then, as the coach finishes talking, speaks up.

"Hey, Rick? We've got a young reporter here from 99.1 FM, a local outlet here in the Ottawa area. Got a question for you."

Here I am. Face to face with Rick Steeves, the coach of the Calgary Flames, who's looking at me and waiting for me to say something.

Something. Anything.

And Josh Drouin, The Legend, is standing there nodding at me, too. Probably regretting that he even tried to include me. And this small group of media looking bored, or unimpressed more likely, waiting for the nobody teen reporter from small-town 99.1 FM to freaking say something so they can get on with their jobs.

"Yeah," I clear my throat. *Think, Griffin. Think about why you're here.*

Nathan McCormick. The look on his face in that hallway ...

"Just wondering about—about McCormick. And bringing him along on this trip. Like, I know he has connections here, but bringing him along with the team when he can't play. Is that something you normally do?"

And that, I realize, is the stupidest question anyone, anywhere, has ever asked. I'll be banned from the Canadian Tire Centre press box. I'm sure of it. I've basically answered my own question—*he has connections here*—but it was all I could drag out of my head, still whirling with that Blair-Evan photo, and MIA Guy, and the McCormick-in-the-hallway movie spinning around.

"Good question," says the coach, and everyone leans in with their phones set to record. "Nathan wanted to come, of course, because he's got connections here, but more importantly, we wanted him to come with us. The team. He's one of us on and off the ice. And yes, he's not playing right now, and that's hard for a young player. Leaving him behind on a road trip while his support team, his friends, his colleagues, go off without him. So yes, to answer your question, he's here because he has some personal connections to Ottawa and Montreal, but most importantly because it's good for a player's health, well-being, recovery from injury. Good to feel part of the team, feel like he might be helping us, even when he can't help us on the ice."

I'd love to see the expression on my face, because I probably look stunned. Which I am.

"Good question," Steeves says again, and he nods toward me before looking around to check there's no more questions, then turns away, back to the dressing room. Scrum over.

Josh Drouin reaches over and gives me a tap on the arm— "Nice job, Griffin. Keep in touch, eh?"—and then he and his camera guy hurry away toward the Senators dressing room.

The reporters trail after Josh down the corridor, phones out, some chatting with each other, all the professionals, doing their job.

But I'm done. I need to get out of here, and I'm already walking in the other direction, texting Jake:

On my way. Meet out front
Still no sign of Guy Martin.

BRIEF MOMENT OF FAME

"Look! Look, Andra! It's Uncle Griffin!"

My sister Claire has the video open on her laptop at the kitchen table and is holding my little niece on her lap, pointing at the screen. Andra squirms, unimpressed, which is about right for a kid who's not even two yet.

Claire is pretty excited, though. She zooms it back to the beginning.

"Listen, Griff! You can just hear you asking the question. See? You're just in the edge of the shot, see? You can see him looking at you."

She's right. I was standing near Josh, and his camera guy turned the lens just enough to catch the top of my head while I was asking the question, mic-less, so not very clearly, thank goodness.

"Mommy, go now," Andra says and squirms off Claire's lap. She toddles to the family room in search of her dad and something, anything more interesting than Uncle Griffin and his moment on Sportsnet.

I listen to the coach's response again and heave a sigh of relief that I came through without embarrassing myself completely.

"Really great, Griff." Claire leans back in her chair and sips her tea. "Awwww. My little bro, the media star."

"Right, that's me." But I laugh, mostly in relief. Also, it's fun to see my big sister cheering me on. After all, she's no slouch herself in the media department, thanks to her job on Parliament Hill.

"You asked a clear question, a meaningful question, and you got a fantastic answer out of him," she says, clicking to another sports site with quotes from the interview. "People in the sports world are loving it. It's the mental health side of it, right? So important. Well done, you."

We're at the kitchen table at her house in Westboro, sharing a pot of tea and waiting for Mom and Dad to show up for a visit and supper. Bella should be here soon, too. I can hear Denis, my brother-in-law, in the family room, playing some game with Andra that involves small fuzzy creatures speaking French and English in funny voices, and hiding all over the room. He's a great dad, Denis.

So here we are. Family. Sunday, late afternoon.

And I'm exhausted. When Jake and his dad dropped me off this afternoon, I actually had to take a deep breath and give myself a pep talk before ringing the doorbell. *Just a few more hours and you'll be on the way home. Finish line in sight. Get through supper and crash in the back seat of the car ...*

"So, who's Rosie?" asks Claire, looking at me over the rim of her cup, eyes all innocent and wide.

"What?"

"Rosie. This girl Rosie, with the little brother. Mom tells me you've been hanging out."

Mom, what the hell??

"They're just neighbors. She's in my class." I shrug, slurp my tea, unsure where this is going. "Her little brother saw me taking shots, so now he's my hockey buddy." I shrug again. "No big deal."

Claire sips and grins at me. "Right."

I give her the look. The *You don't know what you're talking about, Sis* look.

"Mom says you're doing some project with her at the seniors center?"

Everyone seems to be very well informed. I mentioned "the project" once, to Dad, in the car on the way to Jake's on Friday afternoon, when we were catching up on news about the radio station gig and school stuff.

"I am, but I don't have the details yet."

"But it's with this girl. Rosie. Interesting." Claire is grinning at me, waiting for me to rise to the bait and spill more, which I don't.

So, she puts her cup down and says: "How's Blair? I thought you might be spending the day with her today."

"No, she's busy," I say, trying to keep my voice neutral. There is no way I'm getting into this with my sister.

Because my sister doesn't need to know about the texts Blair hasn't replied to, and the phone calls—yes, I do in fact use my phone as a phone sometimes—that went directly to voicemail. *Hi, this is Blair. You can leave a message if you want, and I might even call you back.* I used to think that was funny.

I've looked at that photo of her and Evan at the party about a hundred times, and tell myself that they were just messing with me, just trying to be funny. Show me and Jake what we were missing, great party, whatever.

But now there's this silence. It's all weird. There's a knot in my stomach every time I think of her, and there's nothing I can do about it until she gets back to me. Texts or calls or something.

My phone hasn't left my hand for most of the day. Even here at Claire's kitchen table, it's right there, my fingers curled around it. Pretty sure Claire can see that, too.

"You know, Griff," she says. "You and Blair, and the long-distance thing. It's hard."

I so want to shut this down, because I really don't need

relationship advice from my big sister. And luckily, I don't have to listen to any because, at that moment, the doorbell rings, Andra yells, "GRAMMY AND GRAMPY!" and it's all about greetings and hugs and Andra going nuts, so I just hang in the background.

Waiting for my phone to buzz.

MESSAGES

Earlier on Sunday morning, Jake and I were crashed in his family room, watching Sports Center and getting caught up on last night's scores. I'm pretty sure he notices me checking my phone a lot, but he doesn't say anything.

And when it finally buzzes, I try to be cool and act like I'm dragging my eyes away from the TV to see her name on the screen. Only it isn't Blair.

Guy Martin.

Sorry I didn't get back for the scrum. Saw the video. Nice job

Okay, not overly enthusiastic, but still cool.

Thanks

I wait to see if he's going to say anything else about my moment of fame on CBC. Or maybe tell me where he was last night from the third period on. Or maybe check that I got away from the Canadian Tire Centre okay, like a responsible adult mentor might (well, obviously I did, but he wouldn't know that; he wasn't there).

Nothing. Whatever that means.

"Blair?" asks Jake.

"Nah. Guy Martin."

"The guy missed your moment in the spotlight. Hope he said sorry."

That makes me laugh, because I'm pretty sure Guy doesn't care much about missing my moment in the spotlight. *Nice job.*

So now it's Sunday night after a long day, and I'm in the back seat on the drive back to Glenavon, listening to my parents in the front talking about Bella's announcement that she's been recruited for a job in Calgary. They're discussing the advantages and disadvantages of having a daughter three large provinces away. I'm thinking about the disadvantages of having a girlfriend an hour's drive away. My eyes are closing and I've just about given up on her, when my phone buzzes.

Blair.

That was a crap weekend

I'm so relieved to finally hear something from her that I stop myself from jumping in too quickly with a question about the party picture with Evan. No, I stay cool.

Yeah, it was

Pause to see if she's going to explain, but she doesn't, so I cave:

Sorry

I wait. A minute of nothing while I hold my breath, and then she's typing something ...

Hope you had fun at the game. I mean that. Sorry I was such a bitch

I sigh so loudly in relief, my mother turns around. Smiles vaguely at me and turns back to Dad. "Calgary is a great place to visit, though ..."

It's ok

School dance in November. Can you come?

Quick calculation: school dances are on Friday nights. The trip to that game in Brockville is on a Wednesday, sometime early November. They won't conflict.

Promise

I miss you

We text the whole way home, and once I'm in the privacy of my room, we switch between talking and texting, well past a final bit of homework, my last bowl of cereal, and me falling into bed. I have to sign off, finally, because I'm drifting off between messages. We're both saying all the right things.

Neither of us mentions that photo, though.

RADIO WAVES

"You got to meet McCormick?"

Brad punches my arm on the way to class Monday morning. My good arm, thankfully, but it still hurts.

"Yup." Brad's been chirping at me since he found me at my locker this morning and won't let up.

"I guess it wouldn't have been cool to get a photo with him, eh?"

I have a flashback to the moment in the third period, when I stumbled out into the hallway after Blair's message, to find Nathan McCormick out there, too, leaning on the wall, not looking at his phone, listening to his team getting crushed.

"No, not cool."

My online fame has spread a little, thanks to Guy's Sports Roundup piece on The Legend last night.

Although it's not a serious injury, McCormick was clearly feeling the pain of not being on the ice with his Calgary Flames teammates on Saturday night at the Canadian Tire Centre in Ottawa.

He uses the quote he got at the scrum, and goes on to talk about Nathan's history with the Ottawa 67s, with the World Juniors and his fight with Lars Andersson, the short time at a boarding school in our neighboring town of Brick Hill (where, I found out for the first time, he taught a little kids skills class at the local arena as part of his Hockey Canada penance). Guy found background stuff about his family and junior coach, a girlfriend in Montreal who's a famous musician. It's all good stuff.

And then he ends with two clips:

McCormick's chief concern isn't the injury itself. It's about getting back to doing his job, back where he belongs: "Just wish I could help the team, too."

And the Flames understand this completely. In a response to a question from The Legend's Griffin Tardiff after Saturday's game, Steeves said this:

And he used the quote I got from Steeves, wrapping it up with:

Everyone knows Nathan McCormick will be back on the ice, helping the Flames within the next few weeks. But in the meantime, his coach and teammates have his back until his recovery is complete, and this trip home [meaningful pause inserted here] is a big part of that recovery. This is Guy Martin, reporting for The Legend.

It's the first time I've really heard Guy do anything other than straight game summaries. It's good, like the kind of thing you'd hear on big sports networks. He posted it to The Legend's social media feeds, and it's getting tons of positive responses.

"Nice story," my dad, the Media Studies prof, said this morning when I played it for him off The Legend's website. "And he gave you the credit for that interview, too, which is very professional. Nice work."

So, because I was raised by a mother who drilled good manners into us, I send Guy the appropriate message on Monday morning.

Great report. The press box was fantastic. Thanks for including me

I don't ask if he had a good time with his friends in the stands, of course, or why he didn't follow up with me after the game.

I get a "thumbs up" emoji and:

Hawks home game tomorrow. Can you do a short report? Can just phone it in to Pete. No scrum needed

Sure

I love it. I get to watch a game, write something quick without interviews or the trek to the station and time in front of a microphone.

Another thumbs up, and then this:

Moose game Wednesday in Lancaster. I'm driving. Interested?

Interested, yes. Available, no.

Sorry, can't make that

No prob

Apparently, Elise hasn't told him that I'm already busy on Wednesday night. That's when I'll be at the Avonlea Seniors Lodge, recording interviews with Rosie.

STORIES AT THE AVONLEA

"My father was a fiddle player, in a band. They called themselves The Seanachies, which means the teller of tales in Gaelic. And he was certainly a teller of tales—oh, my. But he was also a farmer."

Mrs. McCrimmon is sitting in an armchair in a corner of the lounge at the Avonlea Seniors Lodge, and you can just tell she was once tall and strong. A farm girl. Her shoulders are a little rounded, sure, and her flowered blouse and bright red sweater hang off her a bit, but she sits up straight, and waves one bony hand around when she speaks, for emphasis. She has no problem finding the words, either. Not doing badly for a ninety-five-year-old.

"So, you heard lots of music when you were a girl, Mrs. McCrimmon?" Rosie asks, lifting her eyes off the large sketch pad on her lap, hand paused over the emerging pencil drawing of the old lady's face.

"Music, always music," Mrs. McCrimmon says. "My mother would sing to the cows in the barn."

I grin and she catches me and winks. This old lady is awesome.

Rosie is doing awesome stuff, too. We've already done two interviews, two sets of drawings. Now I watch her hand as it floats over the page, creating lines, shading, as the face in front of her becomes an image on her page. She does one sketch, talking, pausing, looking up, talking, listening. And then a quick flip of the page and she starts another. Each of the interviews results in three or four sketches.

It's like magic. She's amazing.

The first interview, right after we got set up, was with Mr. Hugh Christie, age ninety-two, a former school principal. He told the story of taking a walk on the railroad tracks as a boy, and nearly getting run over by a train on the trestle over the creek just outside town. Rosie gets him to talk about being small and watching his older brothers go off to war—and what it was like when they didn't come back.

"So sad, Mr. Christie. That must have been so hard." Her pencil pauses, as she looks at him for a moment, then starts again, capturing his long, bony nose, and the flat planes of his cheeks. The pointed chin. His straight mouth that quirks up on one side to show that looking back at the past isn't all sad.

"Harder for my mother, I think. Me, I just kept going to school and dreaming of being a teacher. Doing something worthwhile."

The finished drawings show a strong face, shadows around the eyes, a mouth that seems to want to laugh. She shows them to him.

"Well, here's what I see, Mr. Christie. When you're talking."

He takes a look at the first one, turns the page, turns to the last one, and nods his approval.

"Well now, you've made me more handsome than I am in real life, Rosie," he says, and they grin at each other. It's brilliant.

I sit here off to the side with The Legend's fancy little mic and digital recorder, capturing their words. There, but kind of not there, either. I'm the silent and invisible part of the project, which suits me fine.

It means I get to watch her.

Rosie's doing all the work. It's all between her and these three seniors, who are going to be featured in the museum's local history exhibit. The second interview is with Mme. LaPensée, who grew up in the "funeral parlor" on Main Street, where her father was the undertaker. Oh, man, she has some weird stories about her father's job, but she just laughs about everything.

"Living above a room that usually had a dead body in it," she says. "How did my mother stand it? I do not know." She giggles like a kindergarten kid.

And that all comes through in the sketches Rosie does—the

round face, with eyes crinkled up behind cheeks full of wrinkles but still full and jiggly, the double chin, the curly hair. The smile.

We're nearly done with Mrs. McCrimmon now, and there are sounds and smells coming from the dining room down the hall. Supper time, and we need to wrap up.

Mrs. McCrimmon looks as if she could talk all day, though.

"The cows had to be kept on their schedule, of course. It was always about the cows, and the chores, and the milking," she says. "But my father and his fiddle ... well, the dances at the Bonnie Glen went later than expected sometimes, and he would get home late and have to get up early in the morning. And you know what he would say?"

Rosie has finished her last drawing and is just sitting there, leaning forward, pencil in hand, as if this story is the most important thing in the world.

"What would he say?"

"He would tell us children the next day, 'It was so late when I got home last night, I had to hurry upstairs so I wouldn't meet myself coming down for milking.'" And she bursts out laughing.

"Good one, Mrs. McCrimmon." Rosie laughs, too, and they just sit there smiling at each other. Sharing the moment. I wish I was filming it.

Then Mrs. McCrimmon does something unexpected. She reaches out and takes Rosie's hands, pencil and all, between her own. Squeezes and holds them and looks into Rosie's face.

"You look so like your father," she says. "You are a beautiful girl, Rosie, inside and out."

Everything goes silent as they sit there, joined.

And I feel like an intruder, an eavesdropper, especially since I realize that private moment made it into the interview recording. Slowly, so they don't notice, I hit Stop.

"Ready for your dinner now, Mrs. McCrimmon?"

We all turn at the sound of a bright voice coming from the lounge doorway. One of the Lodge's workers stands there. Dinner time. Time to wrap up.

"Oh, I am, Mary. I'm hungry after all this hard work," says the old lady. One more squeeze and she releases Rosie's hands, smiles at her. "Thank you, dear. That was fun."

"No," says Rosie. "Thank *you*."

SNOW GLOBE

When we step outside, it's snowing again. Like a snow globe, snow softly drifting down under the streetlights.

"Nice," says Rosie, standing on the driveway and turning her face up to let the flakes land on her eyelashes.

I have the urge to take out my phone and snap a picture, but of course I don't, because that would be weird. I like looking at her, though. Girl in a slouchy knitted red toque with a few wisps of dark hair sticking out around her ears and forehead, a knitted red-and-blue scarf wrapped around her neck, its ends trailing front and back over her black coat. She's smiling into the night air, just a little.

Then she opens her eyes and catches me watching her, and the spell is broken. I throw her an apologetic sorry-I-was-staring grin, but she just looks away, adjusts her shoulder bag.

It's a half-hour walk home to Stanley Street, on the other

side of town from the Lodge, and we start off toward the road.

"So, that went well," I say. "As far as I could tell, anyway. Happy seniors, good audio, great sketches."

"I think so. I have some touching up to do on the sketches, but I think they'll be good."

"It's a sort of history thing?" I only know what Elise told me about the project, a joint "memory" project with the museum, radio station, and high school. Old people and young people. Past and present.

"Yes, history. And memory. Remembering what things were like, living here in Glenavon. They're going to have audio playback with headphones. And they'll frame the sketches and display them with old photographs from the museum's archives," she says. "They don't really need the sketches, but Mrs. McAndrews kind of talked them into it. You know," she shrugs, "include the high school kid."

"Hey, your sketches are going to be what people look at first," I say. "I don't know how you do that, draw so quickly. They're great."

She glances at me. "Thanks."

We've reached the end of the street and turn on to the High Street, the main road through town that connects Glenavon with the bigger town of Springbury, closer to the Ottawa River and the bridge over to Quebec. It's busy enough, with cars swishing by in the snow, but the sidewalks are clear, and the streetlights make it easy. We walk along without talking for a while, looking into the windows of the music store, and the kids clothing store, and the florist. And Decarie's Diner, with its windows a little steamy and light streaming out into the snow.

A diner—I wonder. My parents are in Brockville at some meeting and I'm on my own tonight. The recording equipment goes back to the radio station tomorrow, or whenever I go in to edit the audio with Pete.

"Hey, do you have to get home right away?" I ask her and she throws me a look. "I mean, maybe we could have a coffee or something. Or even supper." I nod toward the lighted windows. "At Decarie's."

She looks at me as if I'm speaking a foreign language she doesn't understand. Either that, or she's thinking hard about how to tell me to shut up because, no, she's not going to be seen at Decarie's with Griffin Tardiff.

"I mean, if you're not in a hurry. To get back to Noah, I mean. Or whatever." You would never know this was the star reporter who got Rick Steeves to answer that question in the media scrum at an NHL game. No, I sound like an incoherent loser.

Her phone gives a ring and she pulls it out, takes a quick glance, and stops walking. Holds it up to her ear.

"Hi, Mom."

I feel as if I should keep walking or maybe cover my ears so I'm not eavesdropping, but that's not exactly cool, or easy, so I just stand there watching cars swish by and try to make myself invisible.

"Yup. On my way now." She pauses and I can hear her mother's voice, although not the words. "Yeah, good." She's listening again, then:

"Yeah, Griffin and I are walking home. We're thinking of stopping at Decarie's, though. Is that okay?"

Oh. Okay, then. I glance at her but she's not looking at me.

"Okay. Tell Noah I'll read to him when I get home, okay? Yup. Yup. See you later. Love you."

She slips the phone back in her pocket and looks at me, not with a smile exactly, but not with that closed-off go-away expression she mostly uses around me, either.

"Decarie's," she says, turning toward the diner's front door and glancing over her shoulder at me. "Come on."

JUST HANGING OUT
AT THE LOCAL DINER
WITH ROSIE

"The pain still wakes me up at night."

"But it's getting better, right?"

"Yeah. It's getting better. I have another doctor's appointment in a few weeks, and I'm hoping he'll tell me I can start playing hockey again. Kind of late in the season to find a team, but still."

She's picking at the last of her French fries and not looking at me as she chews slowly. Her hands are small, and clearly she bites her nails. Working hands. Not at all like Blair's. Blair's nails are short, of course (volleyball player ... duh), but perfectly shaped and always painted. Long fingers. Blair could be a hand model.

Why am I thinking about Blair while sitting across the table from this girl?

And why, when Rosie raises her eyes and looks at me, do I have the feeling she knows exactly what I'm thinking at all times?

"Well, I hope you get good news," she says and reaches for another fry.

They know Rosie here, at Decarie's. When we came in, the lady at the till looked up and smiled a huge greeting, and there was a quick and lively conversation about her mom and Noah, as she pointed us toward a booth in the front corner by the window, away from other tables. Like a private seating.

"Your mom working too hard as usual, I bet. Who's your friend?"

Introductions. Mrs. Decarie, the owner's wife. Family diner. New kid in town, Griffin, living in the Pattersons' house for the year. Neighbors. Classmates.

I just sit there and smile politely until we've ordered—"Burger and fries, you have to have that," Rosie tells me. Okay. Sounds good to me—and Mrs. Decarie is gone, and suddenly we're alone, across from each other at a table, without computers or anything between us, except for the salt and pepper and a stand-up flyer, advertising Beer & Wings Night Every Friday.

But it's okay. All okay.

We talk. About Mrs. McCrimmon's story, and Mr. Christie and the train trestle. About school and the best and worst teachers (Dunbar is one of the good ones, we agree). About my move to Glenavon. Eventually we get on to my hockey career, and injury. My old school, my friends. She ignores my one mention of Blair, but actually seems interested as I tell her about Jake and me growing up together at the rink.

"Hockey brothers," she says, and that makes me laugh, because she's absolutely right. "You don't have any brothers or sisters?"

"Actually, I do. Two older sisters."

"Oh," she says, making a fake surprised face. "So, you're the baby of the family."

"I guess. An afterthought, Bella says."

"Bella?"

So, I tell her about Bella and Claire, and Denis and Andra. About my sisters' jobs in Ottawa. About Andra's fixation with Disney movies, the color yellow ("lellow"), and lemurs. How Bella might be moving to Calgary, and I kind of hope she doesn't.

"You'll miss her?"

"I would miss her, yeah."

First time I've ever said that. I find myself telling Rosie how Bella is bossy and a smartass, but she's also always the first one at family gatherings to put me in a headlock, scrub my hair around the top of my head, and tell me to grow up and get a life. How, when she insisted on coming to the hospital after my accident, Jake had to hold her back until our parents arrived, which, according to him, was pretty funny. Bella, my protector.

"She sounds awesome," says Rosie. Reaches for another fry, this time from my plate.

"You have a pretty awesome little brother yourself."

Her mouth curves up in a smile and she nods. "He is awesome. A pain, of course. But awesome."

And then the smile disappears and she glances at me, and I know that we're both thinking the same thing.

This time I'm not missing my chance.

"So, about that night Guy Martin and I showed up at your door."

Another fry from my plate and no eye contact. "Yeah?"

"What was that about?"

She swallows, tilts her head, and looks at me as if I just asked the most stupid question possible.

"You tell me," she says.

"Well, you see, that's it. I have no idea." I wait, but she's staring at me, head on the side, like a teacher waiting for an explanation for some embarrassingly bad behavior. "I mean, the whole idea of helping kids get into hockey was just a random thought I threw out in conversation with Guy weeks ago, and then, without telling me, he drags me along to your house, making it sound like it was a thing."

"He called it a campaign," she says, obviously not impressed.

"Yeah, a campaign. And then suggesting Noah be the poster boy." I shake my head and look at her, adopting the most honestly-I-had-no-idea expression I can muster. Which isn't hard, because that's exactly how I feel. "I didn't know he was going to do that. I didn't even know it was your house, to be honest. I was as stunned as you were when you opened the door."

She looks down, and there's a long moment when she focuses on moving a mushed French fry into the ketchup on her plate, out of the ketchup on her plate. I think we might be getting somewhere, so I wait.

"Pie, kids?"

Mrs. Decarie has appeared out of nowhere, and we both look up at her, startled. It feels a bit like surfacing from a deep dive.

"Come on now, Rosie. I know you love my apple pie," says Mrs. Decarie, sounding exactly like someone's grandmother at a family dinner.

"I do love your apple pie, Mrs. Decarie," Rosie laughs. Looks over at me. "One piece, two forks?"

"Sounds good to me," I nod.

We sit there in silence as Mrs. Decarie gets our pie ready, and I think, *Crap, lost opportunity*. Because it felt like we were opening a door toward something—toward Rosie's story, Noah's story, where Guy fits into all this, and then pie appeared and that was it. Slammed shut.

"Here you go, and Rosie, it's on the house tonight, because I haven't seen you for so long and I want you to come back soon, okay? Bring your mom and Noah." Mrs. Decarie puts this enormous—I mean, like, double-sized—piece of A-1-grade apple pie in front us, plunks the forks down, and winks at me as she turns away.

"Thank you, Mrs. Decarie," Rosie calls to her back, and she waves at us over her shoulder on her way to a table on the other side of the room.

I dig in—because ... pie. And I figure our conversation has probably come to a close, so I might as well get the most out of this experience. Pie will do nicely.

"It's not your fault," she says.

I chew, swallow, wait. Her eyes are on the fork in her hand, but I think it's just because she needs something to look at that isn't my face. Keeping her distance but inching closer.

"Guy Martin is always trying to get in good with my mom, because of what happened to my dad." She glances up quickly, then down again. The fork is getting it all.

"A car accident, I heard. I'm really sorry."

She shrugs. "Yes, a car accident. In the middle of a snowstorm, driving back from Ottawa, where he'd been to a Senators hockey game with Guy Martin. Guy Martin, his best friend."

And then it all comes out in a steady, featureless drone of a voice, as if she's a robot playing back some audio recording.

"Guy Martin and my dad grew up here in Glenavon. They were best friends. Hockey crazy. Like you and your friend Jake," she says, glancing up quickly then back to the fork. "Everybody says Guy might have made it to the NHL, and then he had this injury."

I see Guy and me, leaning on the boards. watching the guys: *An exploded shoulder and a concussion, and that was it for my NHL dreams.*

"My dad wasn't that good, I guess, but he was a really good electrician. Worked all over the region. He was working in Ottawa that week, and Guy convinced him to stay for the game and, of course, they had beers and, of course, it was November and a snowstorm came up suddenly. And a truck skidded out right where my dad's van was skidding out and, all of a sudden, there's the OPP at the door, telling my mom that he's dead."

I'm amazed that fork hasn't melted, she's staring at it so hard.

"I'm so sorry." I want to reach across and touch her. Is that weird? Take her hand, which is clenched on that fork, as she tells me this awful story.

"So, Guy Martin comes along the highway and sees the accident and knows it's my dad's van. And he knows. Him and his hockey game and his beers, and keeping my dad late in Ottawa. So, he knows it's his fault and he's trying to make it up to us. You know, get Noah into hockey. And that internship at The Legend?"

I frown. "My internship?"

"Yeah, your internship. He added that to the list late, on purpose, so that I'd pick it."

231

"What? Why?"

She shrugs and looks down at the fork again. "Mom told him about that first day of school, and me having to leave to pick up Noah, so of course he finds a way to interfere, tells Mom he thought it would be a 'great fit for Rosie.' Not so much doing sports, but just hanging around the station, media, stuff like that. Thought he was doing me a favor. I mean, you saw what the other choices were, right?"

Right. The local cemetery or the seniors residence.

"But you didn't ..." I start, and she shakes her head in disgust.

"Of course I didn't. I don't want his help."

Got it. He's trying to be the helpful family friend. Teach the little kid hockey. Find opportunities for Rosie to do fun media stuff. Take over as father-figure.

She releases her strangle-gaze and clench on the fork, leans forward and puts her hands on to the table, fingers entwined.

"He's kind of a creep," she says very quietly, and then shakes her head quickly, when she sees the effect of those words on me. *Creep* has very specific connotations in a #MeToo world, and she can probably see my imagination spinning out of control by the expression on my face. "No, no. Not *that* kind of creep. He just drinks too much. And he thinks he's so cool, and God's gift to women, including my mother. That's all. He's a pain, and I wish he'd just go away and leave us alone."

A slight quiver on those last words. She's just keeping it together, and I so much want to reach over and cover her hand with mine, show her that I understand. I don't, though. It's probably not a good idea to touch a girl who has just told you about the creepy older guy in her life.

"Okay, I think I get it."

"That night. The night Noah came running to your house," she says, nodding slowly at me to make sure I understand.

And now I do.

"It was Guy. Guy was there with your mother."

She nods.

"Yeah. He does that sometimes. Just shows up. Acts all best friend, sympathetic, supportive, so they open a few beers or the wine, and my mother is such a mess right now. She's exhausted from working shifts at the hospital; she's worried about Noah and his funny reactions to things. She's known Guy since they were kids in school but, shit, she doesn't want to marry him or anything. At least, I hope not." Big sigh. "Sometimes I'm just so tired of all the drama."

"Yeah, I understand. That must be hard." I'm trying to follow advice given to me by Bella, once upon a time, when I was first dating Blair: *Listen to her. Let her know you've heard her. Turn it back to her emotions, not yours. Got it, loverboy?*

"Yeah, it is. And of course, people talk about it, too. Divorced

Guy Martin, widow Judy Courville. Perfect couple." She closes her eyes and takes a deep breath, and when she opens them, she's looking straight at me.

"So now you know why I was so—what did you call it? Stunned?—why I was so stunned when you showed up at our house with Guy Martin. Like you were his little helper."

"Sorry. Really, I'm so sorry. I had no idea about any of this."

She shrugs, leans back in her chair, and there's an awkward silence as I try to think of something to say.

But then—out of nowhere—she smiles, just a half-smile that transforms her face completely and catches me by surprise.

"You should be sorry. You ate that entire piece of pie."

Embarrassing, but true.

WHERE IS THIS GOING?

"They're not getting it, are they?"

I haven't seen much of Guy since he left the press box at the Canadian Tire Centre, now a couple of weeks ago. Some emails about the upcoming road trip, about the high school hockey season. Not much real action, which, honestly, is fine with me.

But this afternoon he shows up at the arena. So now we're standing at the boards, watching the GCI Hawks doing penalty kill drills, and I have to admit, he's right.

"Brad. He's got to isolate the guy in the slot," I say, and I can hear my coach's voice in my head from practices a year ago: *Perimeter, guys. You gotta keep them to the perimeter.*

"Overcommits every time," says Guy. "Look at Bedard. He's about to blow."

Brad is such a good skater, he can actually get away with it— the quick move toward the guy with the puck, then an even quicker readjust to seal off the lane, but Coach Bedard isn't happy.

"Quit showing off, Scott, you moron!" he yells, after blowing his whistle to hit pause.

"So, you're good for the game tomorrow?" Guy asks.

"Yup. All set."

The Hawks have a game in Brockville, which is over an hour away, so the school board has ordered one of the big coaches for the trip. Comfortable seats, video screens—an actual bathroom, like on a train. Permission forms signed and teachers alerted. My first big road trip with the team, and the guys have been giving me the gears about allowing media on the bus.

"No pictures of Murph drooling while he sleeps, right?" Brad tells me.

I assure him there will not be any pictures of Murph or anyone else drooling while asleep.

Mike tells me they mostly play card games.

"They think they're like the big boys," he laughs. "You know, like the Leafs on a plane to the west coast."

"You, too?"

"Nah," says Mike. "I usually just listen to music." He shrugs. "Or sleep. I'm all about having a good time."

Mike and I have been hanging out a bit, playing NHL 14 in his basement, watching the games some nights. He's easy to be around, quiet, smart, knows his way around the whole GCI scene with its weird social groupings. Everybody likes Mike—the guys, of course, but also the girls. He's just a good guy. He reminds me a lot of Jake.

"I'll probably be listening to music and looking out the window," I tell him.

Or maybe I'll be talking shop with Guy, I don't know. Do the media guys sit on their own? Or do we hang out with our own age group?

I guess I'll find out tomorrow.

"Good. I'll meet you at the bus at school, and off we go," says Guy. And then he turns away from the action. "So, listen, I wanted to talk to you about that idea of making organized hockey accessible to more kids."

Right. About time we had this conversation.

"Okay."

"It's a great idea, Griff. Really, it is. But I talked it over with Elise, and I'm not sure this is the best time of year to get that going, you know? With the hockey season already underway? Might be better if we get something rolling next fall, before the season starts. I'm sure you understand."

He's standing there with his hands in the pockets of his leather The Legend jacket, looking at me as if he thinks he's telling me bad news. Like a coach telling me I just got cut from the team. It's weird.

And it occurs to me that he does actually think he's telling me bad news. That he sees himself as the one who's pulling the plug on little Griffin's poorly planned idea.

"Yeah, good. That's fine." I lean on the boards and watch Brad steal the puck and outskate two guys to get a shot on net. Which Murph misses.

"So, you're not disappointed?"

I look at him then.

"Nope. It was just a thought."

Just a thought. Not a big plan that needed to be unveiled at Rosie's front door, freaking everyone out.

"Oh, okay. Great."

He turns back to the practice—Mike makes a great pass to Philip and the penalty kill fails again. Guy and I are silent for a few minutes, and then he speaks, this time without trying to make eye contact.

"And hey, listen, you did a great job in Ottawa at the scrum. I heard from some of the guys, Josh included, that Steeves was really impressed." He turns and nods at me. "That's really something."

"Thanks."

"You know, Griff, I know a lot of those guys. And Josh, of course," he says. "If you want an introduction to anybody, just let me know." He gives my arm a shot and grins again. "You might just have what it takes to join the ranks. Just saying."

"Thanks, thanks a lot," I say and try to look grateful, because it's a nice offer, of course.

"Your dad probably has some connections, too, with his job?"

"No, he's not very involved in the sports scene. His contacts are mostly in the local media circuit, and CBC Ottawa. Maybe a bit of the Parliament Hill press corps, daily news, that kind of thing."

"Well, always happy to help."

"Thanks. I'll keep that in mind if I carry on with media ... and stuff. Thanks." I feel a bit lame, and can't help wondering just what kind of help I could get from someone who kind of messed up weirdly on the hockey-for-kids thing, and then deserted me in the press box at the Canadian Tire Centre a few weeks ago.

"I did it for Josh and look where he is now," Guy says, nodding at me.

Right. Josh Drouin, The Legend.

"And now," he says, pulling his car keys from the pocket of his jacket, "I gotta go."

"Okay. See you tomorrow."

With a wave, he's gone.

I had considered, just for a moment, mentioning the email from Josh, the one I responded to the next day, and Josh's friendly reply: *Keep in touch, Griff. Happy to help you with career advice.*

But I don't. Maybe tomorrow, on the bus. Or maybe it would be better to just keep that to myself.

ROAD TRIP

When Rosie enters the classroom on Wednesday morning, she dumps her books and shoulder bag, and right away walks over to my desk near the window.

Brad's head swivels. Actually, more than one head swivels, along with many pairs of eyes. Rosie doesn't notice, or care, apparently.

"The display is going up at the museum the first weekend of December," she says. No *Hi*. No *Good morning*. Not even a smile. Straight to business. "We're both supposed to be there."

"Great. Okay."

She doesn't say, "Let's go together" or anything. No, she just nods, turns around, and walks back to her desk, still ignoring the gaze of everyone watching this little scene.

Brad catches my eye as she sits down, mouths, "Rosie Courville, eh?" which she can't see from her desk on the other side of him.

I ignore him. Ignore him and everyone else, and the little buzz that went through the room. *Rosie and Griffin?*

I'm looking forward to seeing the display, actually. Rosie's sketches are amazing, and she said there would be old photos and documents as well, and then the audio files that I recorded and delivered to Pete at The Legend 99.1 for editing and uploading onto the special playback units the museum is going to use.

The audio—minus that small moment between Rosie and Mrs. McCrimmon. *You look so like your father. You are a beautiful girl, Rosie, inside and out.*

I managed to erase that little gem because nobody needs to hear that. I'm not even sure I was supposed to hear it.

The morning goes in slow motion. I have trouble focusing on math, or anything, really, which I've noticed is exactly what happens when there's something big coming. Something like a road trip to Brockville on the team bus.

"Gear underneath," Coach Bedard directs the guys, as they lug their hockey bags and sticks out of the school after lunch. "All aboard. Sit anywhere. Lots of seats."

I stand outside watching Brad, Mike, and the guys sling their bags into the storage area and scramble up the steps into the coach. The big, big coach. Lots of jostling inside as they fight over so many seats for no reason at all, other than just to fight each other.

My phone buzzes.

Running late. Will drive. See you there

Guy.

Part of me is surprised. I mean, does this guy not get it? Doing the job as assigned? Sticking to a schedule? Meeting obligations?

But part of me is, to be honest, relieved. I get to hang out with the guys without my—let's face it—kind of weird mentor, supervisor, whatever, in charge of me. I'm on my own.

Another buzz.

Feel free to send out tweets from The Legend account. Newsy stuff. Team on the road

Right, I can do that. I check my phone to make sure I'm logged in to The Legend's Twitter account, and snap a few photos of guys loading their gear. Coach Bedard is still directing traffic, as some of the guys are slow getting to the parking lot.

"Coach?"

He turns and nods at me. "Griffin. Where's your boss?"

"He can't make the bus, so he's driving. Going to meet us there," I say. "So, I just wondered, do you want me to sit at the front? Or ...?"

"Sit anywhere, Griffin. Lots of room," he says and then turns away, distracted by the driver who has a question about something.

Great. I spring up the steps and look for Mike. There, just a few rows back, with an empty seat across the aisle (because no one wants to sit near the front, close to the coaches and teachers, and a couple of rookies, right?).

He sees me, nods. "Griff! Here."

"Hey." I slip into my seat. "Just a sec. Gotta do some work."

I send out a tweet with one of the photos I took.

On the road: Gci Hawks seniors are on their way to Brockville this afternoon. Important game against Brockville Rams. Stay tuned to 99.1 for updates. #GCIHawksHockey #RoadTrip

I text Elise to let her know that I've sent a tweet and will be sending more as the game goes.

Great. Guy there? I'm looking for him

He said he will meet me in Brockville. Driving himself. I'm on team bus

He didn't make the bus?

So, Guy is MIA again, apparently. I pause before answering, because I don't want to get him in trouble. But truth is truth, after all.

No. No problem for me. I'm good on the bus

Okay. Tell him to call me when you see him in Brockville. Tweet out any time. Nothing else on our social media calendar today. Have a good trip. Thanks!

Will do

And then a quick text to Mom, as agreed, because yes, I'm that teenager who still checks in with his mom.

On the road. All good

Thumbs up from Mom. And then I see she's typing something.

Dad's in Brockville today for a meeting. Said he might come up to the game

Crap. That means he'll expect me to drive home with him. No team bus back to Glenavon. Before I can answer, Mom's typing again.

Relax. He won't mind if you take the bus home

Yeah, my mother totally gets me.

So, once that's done, I figure I can relax and enjoy the ride. And I plan to enjoy it because, after all, it's been a while since I've been on a team bus. Guys talking loudly, especially the guys at the back. (Question: Why do the loudest guys always take over the back of the bus?) Coaches at the front, of course. A couple of rookies have taken over the seats in front of Mike and me, speaking French. Some guys are watching the video screens for the trip-approved entertainment to start—some series that's plugged into the DVD player at the front of the bus.

"Where's Guy Martin?" Mike asks, as we pick up speed.

"He's driving. Couldn't make the departure time, I guess."

Mike grins. "Sounds like Guy." And when I look at him, questioning, he adds: "Haven't you noticed that Guy Martin kinda likes to do his own thing?"

Do his own thing—is that what it's called? But I just grin and nod in agreement. I don't want to talk about Guy Martin.

"So, what are your chances today? Are they a good team, the Rams?"

And we talk hockey for a while, as the bus makes its way through all the small towns on the road that leads to the highway. The snow-covered farmers' fields and bush lots slide past. Barns, silos, then another town, each one with about four churches, a sketchy tavern, and even a *French Fry Capital of Canada/Capitale de la Patate-Frite du Canada* sign.

"Oh, man, I have to go there," I tell Mike, my head swiveling as I clock the name of the town.

"The best. I'll go with you."

I'm glad Mike chose to sit closer to the front, because the noise seems to increase the farther we travel.

"You cheated! No way that's your hand." Brad's swatting at Murph, and two other guys are laughing.

"Are you kidding me? Ryan has Marchand all day." Philip and some of the senior players, discussing the Senators chances against Boston this weekend.

I look out the window at the scene sliding by. The clouds have started to wash out the sun, and everything seems to be changing color, changing texture out on the land, as one of those early winter cloud banks rolls in from over Lake Ontario.

It reminds me of my last road trip, to the OFSAA playoffs, sitting with Jake, and I just couldn't wait to get out on the ice and play that Owen Sound team. Turns out I should have waited, I guess.

"It's been a while since I've been on a team bus," I say to Mike, feeling like a kid, and glad I'm sitting here across the aisle from him. Relieved, actually, that I'm not sitting with Guy Martin on this bus and obligated to act like a media guy.

Mike nods, smiles at me.

Yeah, today I feel like part of the team again, and it feels good.

AND THEN ...

It happens so fast—the sudden lurch, the shift in gravity as my body pitches into the air and comes down hard. The voices raised in surprise, unfamiliar clunks and bangs and scrapings. More voices—yelling, scared. Someone shouts in pain.

I was asleep, dreaming of skating down the Rideau Canal with a stick in my hands, all powerful and smooth and pain-free, and no sound but the wind and my skate blades—and then I wake up feeling the universe tilt on its side, and I grab the tops of the seats on either side of me as Mike lands on me and pins me to the floor. No, not to the floor—to the window underneath me.

What's happening?

When I fell asleep a while ago, the bus was leaving the little takeout diner in Brockville in the dark, snow swirling around and the wind picking up, but nothing to worry about, the driver said. The guys had just won their game, a close one, a beauty, actually, and they were pumped, but takeout food and the effort must have caught up to everyone because, once the bus is rolling, it gets quieter. Hum of the wheels on the highway, hum of conversation, especially Brad, who apparently doesn't have an OFF switch.

But it's all good, and I'm sitting across from Mike and yawning. Job done. Tweets and a game report sent. On my own because, weirdly, Guy never showed up. Something came up, he texted. Have to sit this one out. You got it, Griff. Let me know if you need back-up on social media. It occurs to me that maybe he did this on purpose, to give me a shot at doing it on my own, so I could enjoy the team bus experience by myself. But then I think, *No way*. He likes to be where the action is, but maybe this just wasn't enough action for him.

There's sure enough action right now. That sudden swoop through the air and a hard landing.

"Shit!" Mike says, and his voice is high and scared. "You okay?"

We scramble to find our bearings, find some space in the dark bus so that he's not squishing me. He pushes himself off me, using the seat backs, and his hand slips and he crushes my arm and shoulder for a minute. Pain sears down my arm and I try not to cry out. There's enough crying out going on already.

"I'm okay. What happened?"

"Guys!" Coach Bedard, somewhere near us in the gloom.

No lights, no engine hum. His voice is shaky. "Guys! Stay where you are."

"Brad's hurt!" Murph calls from the back. He might be crying, actually. Other guys are making noises.

"Stay where you are. We're going to get everyone off the bus. We just hit some ice and rolled over into the median. Guys, stay where you are, and we'll do this so everyone's okay. You listening? You hear me?"

There's a rough response of voices calling, *Okay, coach. Yeah.* Also a fair bit of swearing. Maybe some groaning. Someone's crying in pain.

"Bradley Scott, can you hear me?"

"Coach." Yes, it's Brad who's crying.

"Stay put, son. All of you, stay put. We'll get everyone out, but we've got to go carefully, okay?"

Another chorus of voices. People are starting to calm down a bit now.

Mike and I have managed to pull ourselves into a half-standing position, our feet on the window that's pressed against the ground. There are a few of us, heads poking up and looking around.

"You okay?" Mike asks me. "Sorry about the arm."

"I'm okay," I tell him, and I am. I flex my arm, rotate my shoulder. Nothing major, as far as I can tell. "How do we get out?"

"You boys at the front here, Marc, Sylvain." The two rookies in the row in front of us. "Mike, Griffin. Can you climb up to the front here? We can get you out the door if you can climb up here."

So we do, the two guys in front of us, and then Mike and me, like climbing some weird piece of playground equipment. Over a few rows of seats, and there's Coach Bedard and the assistant coach (also Math teacher), Mr. Somerville, ready to help as we clamber down the bus steps—kind of like a bridge now—and jump down with the help of the driver, whose hand is shaking a little as he reaches up to steady me.

And we're in a blizzard. Where did that come from? I've seen it before, of course. A familiar crazy weather event that anyone who lives in the Ottawa Valley or near Lake Ontario recognizes. That cloud bank from earlier turned into a monster whiteout, looking for some fun along the 401. And we must have driven right into it.

"Stay on this side of the bus, boys," the driver says. Yeah, his voice is shaking a little, too. "You'll be out of the worst of the wind here. Just stick together, okay?"

So we do. The four of us huddle together along the side of the coach, which, since it's on its side, is actually the bottom, big wheels sticking out and the mechanical underbelly still giving off a bit of welcome warmth.

Sylvain swears in the best colorful francophone style and we all giggle, sounding like a bunch of over-excited middle-schoolers. My legs are shaking, and suddenly I'm a little kid, wanting my parents.

Dad. He didn't show up at the arena, so he must still be at work at the campus in Brockville. Or else he's on this highway right now, too.

I pull out my phone and call him. (My fingers are shaking. Why are my fingers shaking?) No answer.

Call Mom. She answers on the first ring.

"Hey, how was the game?"

"Mom? We—we had an accident." My voice is shaking now, too. Cold, shock. *Shit. I'm not going to start crying, am I?*

"What? Griffin, where are you?"

Good question. "The bus rolled over on the median." I look at Mike and ask, *Where are we?* He shrugs, looking as blasted as I feel.

Sylvain answers. "We're just east of the Ingleside exit. I saw the sign just before we went flying."

So I tell her, and she says a whole bunch of stuff about staying together. Following instructions. Just stay calm; it's all going to be okay, Griffin. You're not hurt? Good. Stay with your friends and help will come.

I start to hear and see clearly again. It's going to be okay. Mom is working her magic.

"Okay, Griffin? You're okay, just stay together, and I'm sure help will be there soon."

Sirens. Through the howl of the blizzard, the other sounds coming from the bus, as the guys inside are clunking their way through the weird playground to the front door, we hear sirens.

"Sirens," I manage to say. She's right, as always. Help is coming. "I can hear sirens now."

"Good. Stay put, Griffin. I'll see you soon. Keep your phone handy, okay?"

"Dad—have you heard from Dad?"

"Calling him now."

A few more words and we click off. I feel a bit calmer now, and hope Mike and the guys didn't hear the panic in my voice. Probably not. Guys are pulling out their phones and making their own calls, texts. Nobody listens, but it doesn't matter. You can't really hear over the wind, anyway.

So, yeah, I'm calmer. Also colder. A few more guys have joined us in our survivor huddle, and we stay close, looking through the snow at headlights of other vehicles. A transport truck, judging from the multiple lights along the side, jackknifed across the highway. Smaller vehicles. Everyone pointed in different directions. We're not the only vehicle in the median, but there are lights and distant sounds, and voices coming through the howl of the wind.

"What happened?"

We talk among ourselves, huddling together for warmth.

The snow when we left Brockville, the blizzard, a whiteout. Sylvain and Marc say they could see brake lights swerving all over the road in front, and then the sound of the bus's brakes and everything going into orbit, and here we are.

The sirens get louder. Flashing lights of emergency vehicles, police.

"You okay?" Mike asks me, once he's finished calling someone, his parents, I guess, I don't know.

"Yeah, I think so. Shakes you up, eh?"

"Yeah." He's quiet for a moment, his eyes on the door of the bus, where Philip is jumping down, helped by the driver. Another guy right after him. "Brad sounded bad. I hope he's okay."

"Yeah." I look around and see that most of the team is out of the bus now, part of the huddle.

"He can be a dick, I know, but he's probably the strongest guy on the team, physically," says Mike. "He sounded hurt in there."

We look at each other in the weird flashing lights of the emergency vehicles, both of us worrying about Brad, and listening to sirens through the wind, and wondering what comes next.

ON THE JOB

What comes next is a call from Elise.

"Griffin? You okay? I just heard on the police scanner that there's an accident on the 401. Where are you?"

Well, that didn't take long.

"Standing on the median of the 401 beside our bus. On its side. Yeah, we were in the accident."

"Oh, my God! Are you okay?"

"I'm fine," I say, and realize that I am. I really am. We're sheltered from the wind and the snow has stopped. I can see stars.

"Anyone hurt?"

"Looks like bumps and bruises. Maybe Brad Scott ... he's not off the bus yet."

"Okay, Griffin, do you think you're up to sending me some photos? Maybe doing a quick report over the phone?"

So, this is life in the media. You get tossed around a bus, and end up standing in the middle of the 401 in the cold, and your boss wants a scoop.

"Sure. What do I ...?"

She gives me some instructions—just text her the photos and she'll add hashtags and tags to help spread out the social media notifications: CBC, another Ottawa radio station, a TV station. A few sentences about the scene—"Okay? I'm recording—just describe what you see"—and I hope my voice isn't shaking. Actually, it feels good to have something to focus on.

Standing beside the team's overturned bus ... there's a transport truck jackknifed across the eastbound lanes ... cars and trucks back up behind us ... emergency vehicles ... team is mostly out of the bus and standing together, waiting for instructions ...

I hardly know what I'm saying, just calling it like I see it unfolding around me.

"That's great," she says. "Now send me some photos and keep your phone close, okay? I might need more. Great job, Griff. You're okay?"

"I'm okay. Call me back if you need anything. I'll take some photos now."

I get to work snapping pictures of the overturned bus, without showing any of the guys (she didn't say that, but I just think none of the parents back in Glenavon will want to see their sons standing there huddled against a bus's underbelly like a bunch of cows in a farmer's field). The lights down the highway, including the red and blue of the emergency vehicles. A cop is talking to our driver now, so I snap that, too—an action shot.

I check that the photos are okay and send them to her. It's slow, but we're actually near a communication tower and my data seems to be strong. I check my battery—still lots of juice.

"On the job?" asks Mike when I come back to the huddle, and I nod.

"Any sign of Brad yet?"

He shakes his head. "Murph either. Coach and Mr. Somerville are still in there with them."

I check my phone, out of habit more than anything, and scroll to The Legend 99.1 Twitter account.

Elise works fast, apparently:

BREAKING NEWS: *Scene from accident during whiteout on eastbound 401 east of Ingleside exit. GCI Hawks hockey bus involved. Photos by Griffin Tardiff*

The photos are pretty dramatic, grouped together under the tweet's content. Even in still photos, it looks as if everything is in motion, as if you can see the wind whipping the snow around and the lights flashing on the first responders' vehicles. And then the bus, multiple wheels with those big tires sticking up sideways into the air.

The cop is on his radio now, and looking at us.

"Help is on the way, I think," Sylvain says, and everyone turns to see a couple of the ambulance attendants heading our way, carrying equipment bags. A quick conversation with the driver and they climb up into the bus with help from the cop and the driver.

Mike and I look at each other: Brad.

"Hey, guys," calls the cop, coming toward us now. He's big and reassuring, and we all kind of drift toward him without thinking. "Come on, let's get you somewhere warm, okay? We've got a school bus down the road a ways. Everybody can walk? Any injuries? No? Good. We'll get you warm and have somebody check you out. Come on."

We're walking along the shoulder of the road now, past cars with their engines running, waiting to be directed around the transport truck that's blocking the highway. Eyes watch us go by, this herd of hockey players, all of us hunched over against the cold. But just beyond the truck, we can see the lights of a school bus. A warm school bus. The cops must have had it brought in from Cornwall for us. Man, a school bus never looked so good.

I'm just thinking about calling Mom again when my phone buzzes. A text from Elise.

Cʙᴄ Ottawa wants to interview you. Up for it?

"Shit," I say, loudly enough for Mike and Sylvain to turn and look at me. I wave them off. "No, it's okay."

257

Sure

Stay tuned. I'll be in touch with details.

Then she adds, another text:

You ok?

I send her the thumbs up.

"Here you go, guys," says the cop, as we arrive at the bus and the driver creaks open the doors for us. "Come on up and get warm. I'll just check on the rest of your group and someone will let you know what's next. Just wait here for us, okay?"

Fine with us. Everybody scrambles on and finds a seat.

"Well, it's not fancy," says Sylvain, loud enough that everybody can hear. "But I think it'll do, eh, guys?"

General noise as conversations start up and the guys start to relax, pull out their phones, call people—parents? Girlfriends? Maybe I should call Blair? Or Mom again? No, because I'm waiting for Elise—and there it is.

Josh Drouin will call shortly. I gave him your number. Just wants you to answer a few questions for news report. Okay?

Thumbs up.

I sit there, watching my phone, waiting for it to ring. I'm afraid to take my eyes off it in case I miss the call. Yeah, my big chance to get interviewed by Josh Drouin—not because I was a star in a hockey game, but because our bus went off the road in a snowstorm. Not exactly news, is it ...?

My phone lights up as the call comes in.

"Hello?"

"Hi, Griffin. Josh Drouin here. I hear you're having some excitement there on the road trip to Brockville?"

"You could say that, yeah."

We chat a little bit and I know he's just trying to ease me into the call. Maybe testing levels. He checks with me to make sure I'm okay being interviewed, that it's just a news piece. He's taking it because of the local hockey angle. Good with me? Yeah, sure, good.

It's easy. He does a sound check, then a long silence, while we wait for the cue from his producer, then he launches into it.

"We have Griffin Tardiff on the line from the scene of the accident this evening on the eastbound 401 near Cornwall. Whiteout conditions just after six o'clock sent a tractor-trailer spinning across the highway, and a bus carrying the Glenavon Hawks senior hockey team was forced onto the median and rolled over. First, Griffin, are you okay?"

"I'm fine, yeah. No injuries."

"And can you describe where you are right now?"

So I do. I talk about the bus, being warm, finally, after hanging outside for a half-hour or so. Mike is grinning at me from across the aisle, and when somebody at the back starts talking loudly, the guys at the front shush him—*Griff's on the radio!* Oh, great, now they're all listening.

But it's easy, really, because Josh makes it easy for me. Questions about the road conditions, first reactions to the accident, how we got out of the bus. Waiting in the cold until the nice cop came along, and the walk down the side of the highway to reach our little safe space here. A couple of guys still in the bus with paramedics (he doesn't ask me to identify anyone, which I think is a good call). Yes, we had stopped for something to eat in Brockville after the game. Yes, the Hawks won. Looking forward to getting home.

I hope he didn't notice that my voice caught a little on that last part.

And then we're done. A pause of about five seconds, then I hear Josh say something to someone, maybe on another phone? Is he in a studio? I don't know.

"Hey Griff, great job. Just what we were looking for. I know that probably wasn't easy under the circumstances, so thanks for that little scoop. You okay?"

We chat a little and he tells me the spot will go out shortly on the evening news, and it will probably play later tonight, too. Good work. Keep in touch. Get home safe.

I finish the call and put my phone down. I'm exhausted.

"Nice," says Mike. "Making us famous."

I'm about to reply when the door of the bus opens and we all look up, expecting Coach Bedard. But it's not Coach. It's the nice cop who steps up into the aisle and turns to someone following him.

Dad.

SAFE

My phone is blowing up, and there's so much stuff rattling around in my head right now, that I'm tempted to just turn it off and toss it into the back seat. Of course, Mike would probably just toss it back at me, so I sit up and try to focus on who I should reply to first: Mom, Blair, Jake, or Elise? Oh, and there's also Bella and Claire. And a couple of guys from my old school in Ottawa. And Murph, who finally made it back to the warm school bus with Mr. Somerville, once the paramedics got Coach Bedard and Brad loaded into the ambulance. Brad and his dislocated shoulder, poor guy.

I missed seeing Murph, though. I was allowed to leave, thanks to having a parent show up. A parent with a car parked on the shoulder of the road just up ahead.

"Mom called when I was just past Long Sault, so I got off at the Power Dam Road exit and turned around and came back," Dad explained once we were underway. "The cops were great, once I explained to them that you were one of the kids on the bus."

He'd had to do some fancy driving, too, crossing the median on one of those Do Not Enter cops-only access roads between the two sides of the divided highway, and then driving the wrong way—illegally—down the empty eastbound lanes until he got to the start of the pile-up, where the emergency vehicles and our rescue school bus, and a very irate OPP constable confirmed he'd arrived at the right spot.

My dad, the rebel. So proud of him. Also grateful for the rescue.

At first, the nice cop on the school bus wasn't going to let anyone come with us, but Mike made a quick call to his mom for confirmation and got the green light from Mr. Somerville. The rest of the guys were okay with it, cracking jokes about half-milers, wimps, traitors, but since Mike had just scored a goal and had three assists in their 4-3 win, no one could really complain. And besides, the bus was warm, and the cop told them they'd be leaving very shortly.

So, now we're back cruising down the 401, heading home. The stars are out, and it's warm in the car. Safe. After a whole lot of talking as we first got underway with Dad—"Oh, man, it was nuts. Guys flying everywhere. And Brad. And we had to climb over the seats. Did you know that kid Sylvain was such a comedian? It was cold, but we were out of the wind, at least ..."—Mike and I kind of run out of gas and stop blabbering. Dad just drives and doesn't ask us any big questions, lets us talk. He reaches over and squeezes the back of my neck. "Glad you got through it okay," he says.

I tell him quickly about the interview with Josh, but just briefly, and he hasn't heard it yet. Later I'll find it online for him, but for now, it's everyone else who wants to talk about it.

Which is why my phone is blowing up.

Jake: Heard you on CBC. Fun road trip?

Mom: YOU WERE ON CBC!!!! At least I know you're OK

Bella and Claire, the guys from school, checking in, asking questions.

And Elise: Nice work, Griff!

Murph: Got back to the bus after you guys left. Brad has dislocated shoulder. Maybe concussion—and then a whole lot of swear words and emojis.

And Blair: MOM HEARD YOU ON THE RADIO. ARE YOU OK?? Followed by a long back-and-forth exchange that I have to be careful with, not wanting to mix up my replies. I mean, my mother does not need to receive a message intended for my girlfriend's eyes only, right?

And it's just when I'm nearing exhaustion point, when I think that's it, time to turn off this phone and stare out at the highway, and the stars, and be quiet and still for a few minutes, maybe stop the buzzing in my head that's filled with images of the wrong-way-up bus, and the sound of Brad Scott crying in pain somewhere back there in the dark—that's when the text comes from Guy.

You ok?

I thought I'd hear from him sooner. Thought maybe Elise would have been on to him. Thought he might have heard the interview. Who knows what I thought about Guy Martin.

All ok. On my way home with my dad

Long pause, and I think maybe I can bail now, but then I see him typing something, and after a minute:

I should have been there

I don't know how to reply to that because, yes, he should have been there, but then he would have been thrown around the bus, too, and that's not great.

Just an accident

Long pause, then:

I've seen my share of accidents. Glad you're okay

Thanks

He's typing something and I wait, wishing this conversation was over, because it occurs to me that he might actually be thinking about a different accident, on a different snowy highway, with a different ending. The night Rosie's dad died.

The typing stops, starts, stops. After a few minutes of staring at the screen, no message. I turn off my phone and lean my head back against the headrest. Close my eyes.

I wonder if Rosie knows I was in an accident on the highway tonight.

RESCUE

I'm stuffing my face with Mom's apple crisp. Apparently, this is what she decided to do, as soon as Dad called to let her know he had retrieved me and Mike from the bus and we were on our way home. Baking. The cure for everything.

And it's working. We took Mike home, and now we're sitting around the kitchen table, Dad with a beer, Mom with tea, me with hot chocolate and apple crisp—yes, I may be channeling my inner twelve-year-old. It's nearly nine o'clock and I'm starting to fade, but my mom's apple crisp must be dealt with first.

"So, your arm feels okay?" she asks.

"Yeah, it's fine," I mumble through a mouthful.

"Even though Mike landed on you?"

"Even though Mike landed on me." I give a huge shrug, rotate the arm a few times. No pain. "Maybe he fixed it."

They're just smiling at that when the doorbell rings, followed by wild thumping. Like two hands pummeling the door. We're all up out of our chairs in a second, but it's Dad who gets there first.

Noah. Face contorted with fear, tears.

"Rosie's yelling at Mom! The guy is there again, and Mom is crying!"

"Come on in here, son, you're safe here." Dad puts his arm around Noah's shaking shoulders and draws him in, but Noah sees me and bolts right into my stomach.

The guy. Guy.

"Hey, bud, it's okay. You're safe here. We'll help." I hold him in a hug and look at my parents.

The kid has hands like claws, digging into my back, and he's shaking like crazy.

"Rosie was yelling ..."

He's crying now. I look at my parents, and they're doing that thing parents do, the silent conversation that happens magically so that kids don't hear. But I hear.

Dad: Keep him here.

Mom, reaching out to touch Noah's back: Got it covered. Go fix this.

Dad, looking at me: You know what's going on, don't you?

But out loud, he says:

"Hey, Noah? Why don't you stay here with Griffin's mom, and we'll go help Rosie and your mom, okay? You're safe here, son."

"Come on, Noah," Mom says in her softest, soothing voice—the one I've heard her use on Andra, maybe even on me, once upon a time—"We'll go make you some hot chocolate and curl up on the couch. I bet we can find some hockey to watch. Come on, buddy. You can let go of Griffin. He'll be back soon. You're okay."

Yeah, the magic works, as always. Noah moves into the circle of my mother's arm and lets her lead him away, but he looks back at me, still gulping with tears after what was probably a breathless mad dash in the dark and cold from his house.

"You'll be back soon?"

"I'll be back soon, and we'll watch some hockey," I say. "You go with my mom and I'll go get Rosie, okay? It's all going to be okay, you'll see."

He doesn't have any more words. Just turns, gulping and sniffing, and heads back to the kitchen with Mom.

"Let's go," says Dad, getting our jackets out of the front hall closet. "You'll have to direct me."

It's a short drive, but it's long enough to fill him in. I tell him the condensed version of what I know about the Courvilles and Guy Martin, the weird relationship, Rosie hating him showing up at the house.

"He's not a bad guy," I say, and wish I'd had an opportunity to tell Dad more about the weird night he dragged me along to Rosie's house. Or about disappearing from the press box. Or the general comments about "Oh, Guy" that I keep hearing from people—Mike, Josh, Elise.

"But ...?" My Dad can tell there's something.

"Turn here, this white house, with the black suv in the driveway." I direct him, and it's easy, because Guy's flashy suv is hard to miss.

"But ...?" Dad says again, once we're parked. "He's not a bad guy, but ...? I feel there's something you're not telling me."

What should I say that Dad would understand?

"It's like he thinks he's more important than he is," I say, staring at Rosie's front door and wondering what's going on in there. "It's like he thinks he's some boss. Thinks he's cool. The guy who makes things happen." Maybe he is. He made things happen for me, with the reporting for The Legend, the press box at the Senators game, introducing me to Josh Drouin, right? "I guess he thinks he can make things right for Rosie's mom, too."

My head is like a movie screen, full of images. That night Noah came running to our house in the dark. And the night we showed up at their door like we were going to save Noah by making him the poster boy for the hockey campaign.

And Rosie's voice: *Not that kind of creep. He just drinks too much. And he thinks he's God's gift to women, including my mother. That's all. He's a pain, and I wish he'd just go away and leave us alone.*

But other thoughts are crashing around in my already crashed-out head, too. Today's missed road trip. That overheard conversation with Elise in the hallway ...

"You don't think we should be calling the police?" Dad asks me, and I glance over quickly, shaking my head. "He's not violent, or dangerous to Rosie or her mother?"

"No, no, I'm sure he's not. It's not that. It's just ..." I look at the door again, the light in the windows. "I don't know, he's just kind of ... a jerk."

Dad sighs and reaches for the door. "Well, come on, Griff. Let's ride to the rescue, if we can."

I have to ring the doorbell twice, which freaks me out a bit, thinking there's some reason no one can come answer it, but then we hear steps and there's Rosie.

I can tell she's been crying, eyes red and lashes a bit matted, and she's momentarily shocked to see us. Probably especially shocked to see Dad, because I realize she's never met him before.

"Hey," I say quickly, before she can do anything. Like slam the door in our faces. "Noah's at our house." Her face goes white, eyes widen—she didn't know. "We came to see if we can help. This is my dad."

And then Dad takes over.

"Hi, Rosie. Can we come in?"

She automatically steps back, because my dad has that effect on people, something about his calm voice that makes people react, move. He lets me go first, still talking.

"Noah was quite concerned, so we said we'd just come make sure everything's okay with you and your mom. Where is your mom, Rosie?"

She hesitates, her eyes flicking to me, but then she points to the living room just off the front hallway, and we all turn and look.

Mrs. Courville is standing in front of a chair, as if she just stood up, watching us, embarrassed. Guy Martin is there, too, but he's passed out on the couch. Table with glasses, beer cans, a full ashtray.

Dad and I stand there, taking it all in, and then he says in that quiet, calm, in-charge voice that he's so good at:

"Griffin, why don't you take Rosie back to our house now? Rosie? Got your coat handy?"

"But ... Mom?" Rosie looks at her mother and then looks back at us, says in a strangled voice—and I realize she's shivering, very close to tears: "I should stay."

Dad smiles at her.

"Don't worry about your mom. I'm going to drive her back to our house, too, in a minute. But why don't you and Griffin get a head start. It's a lovely night out there for a walk, and I'm sure Griffin's mom will have the hot chocolate going. Okay?"

The spell is working, my dad's voice. I guess it's not just my mom who's a wizard. Rosie glances at her mom, who nods, gives her a smile of encouragement. She goes back down the hallway toward the kitchen, and comes back with her coat, hat, scarf.

"Help her, Griff," Dad says. "There you go."

I hold her coat for her, and would be happy to do up the zipper, too, since her hands are shaking so much. She manages, somehow, though, and then the hat, the scarf, not looking at me. "Okay, kids? We'll be there in a minute. Probably pass you on the road."

"Come on," I say, and she follows me.

A quick look back at my dad. He nods at me and closes the door behind us.

UNDER THE STARS

At first, we don't talk. We just walk. Not too fast, but steady. The wind is behind us so it's cold, but not too cold. Not biting. A good night for a walk, and I realize that after everything that's happened today, this actually feels good.

Above us, the sky is clear and, after a while, I look up at the stars.

I glance over at her and see tears sliding down her cheeks.

"Hey, it's okay," I say, and she turns to me, face crumpling, so I do what I have to do and wrap my arms around her, while she sobs into my shoulder. I have a momentary thought that our parents might drive by any minute and see us, which would perhaps lead to questions. But no. No cars pass. Just a bit of wind in the branches of the tallest trees, a creaking light standard up ahead. And the stars.

After a minute or so, she pulls away and rubs her face.

"Sorry."

"It's okay."

We start walking again.

"He told us you were in an accident," she says after a few minutes of silence. "Are you okay?"

"Yeah, I'm fine. Mike landed on me, and I thought my arm might have been set back a few months, but no. All good." I glance at her and she actually smiles at that. "Brad Scott got hurt, though. Dislocated shoulder."

"Oh, that's bad."

"Yeah." No need to describe the sounds of Brad crying at the back of the bus in the dark.

"That's why he came over, you know. Because he was messed up over your accident."

I know right away who she's talking about. She doesn't wait for me, but goes on, her voice flat, tired.

"He said he had a job interview, but he didn't want to tell Elise Rogers. Some big online sports thing, some woman he knew offered him a job, so he had an interview, but he hadn't told Elise, so he couldn't go to the game on the bus. And then the snow, and the accident, and he said it was like Dad all over again."

I just let her talk. Her voice is starting to creep up a little, as if her throat is closing, the way it does before you start crying.

"He just showed up at the door, all agitated, and Mom let him in, and then the beers started flowing and it got all emotional, and he said he'd screwed up again."

She's in full flow now, voice breaking, tears starting. We're at my house now, but I don't want to take her in the front door when she's like this, so I lead her up the driveway and around to the back, where we can go in through the garage to the mud room. She can calm down before she has to face anyone.

"He was so worried about you, Griffin. And then I just got so mad, as if he'd just deserted you and the other guys. Doing his own thing, thinking about what's good for him, like always. And then Mom started being all motherly and sympathetic, because that's all she knows how to do, and I got mad at her, too. I yelled at her. I yelled at my mom."

She's sobbing again, so I hold her again, just outside the garage side door, in the dark.

"It's okay." I keep saying it over and over, into her red slouchy hat, hoping she can hear me.

The hum of the garage door opener and flash of headlights in the window beside us, but we're here in the dark where no one can see us.

"They're back," I say, but she's still crying.

I hear the car doors open, and my dad:

"We'll go in this way. Give you a minute to catch your breath. I'm sure Lisa will have the kettle on."

And Mrs. Courville:

"You're being very kind, Don. I feel awful about imposing on you like this."

The car doors clunk shut, and they go up the step and into the mudroom, my dad replying: "You're not imposing. We're happy to help. You go on in, and I'll drive your visitor home, okay?"

The mudroom door closes and, after a moment, I hear Dad come back out, get back in the car, and drive away. Garage door goes down. It's quiet again.

"You ready to go in?" I whisper in her ear. Or at least where I think her ear is.

She nods, so we disentangle and I lead the way in the side door, through the garage, still lit from the opener. Open the door into the mudroom, which is dark and deserted. The door leading to the kitchen is partly open, and we can hear Mom and Mrs. Courville. We can't see them, so they must be standing in the hallway between the kitchen and family room, where Noah is.

"See? Noah's asleep on the couch, so don't worry about him, Judy." Mom, using her reassuring voice. "And I'm sure Griffin will have Rosie home soon. You can trust Griffin. They're probably just walking. Walking and talking."

Silence, and then Mom again. "Judy. It's okay, hon. It's okay."

"Your son is such a great kid." It's Mrs. Courville, and she's crying.

Rosie goes still, then puts her hand to her mouth, as if smothering all the things she wants to say.

"You have two pretty great kids, too," says my mom. "They look after each other, and they look after you. Who could ask for more?"

A shaky laugh and, "You're so kind."

"You're doing a great job," Mom says, gently.

"They are my life."

Then silence.

I don't know what's happening out there—maybe the two moms looking at each other and crying, maybe they're hugging. Maybe they've moved on to the family room and Noah.

But here, in the dark mudroom, Rosie turns to me and buries her head in my shoulder again, arms around my waist, tight. As if she can't face anything on the other side of that door and is holding on to me because I'm her life raft.

That's okay with me. I'm happy to stand here in the dark mudroom, holding Rosie, because I've just realized something.

Holding Blair never felt like this.

PHONE,
PART ONE

Mom lets me stay home on Thursday, which is great, because it was late by the time Rosie and Noah and their mom left. It was even later when Mom and Dad got back from delivering Guy's car back to his place so Mrs. Courville wouldn't have to deal with that—or give the neighbors something to talk about. And it was later still when Mom and Dad and I were finally able to have a quick debrief in the family room, where I'm sprawled on the couch, trying to keep my eyes open and focus.

"I had to shake him awake," Dad tells us. "He was in pretty bad shape, had trouble understanding who I was at first. But once I got through to him that Judy and the kids were not there and it was time to go, he just seemed embarrassed."

"As well he should be!" Mom is sipping on wine now, because tea is obviously not strong enough to deal with this kind of drama. "Imagine showing up like that. Poor Judy!"

"Well, he said he was feeling pretty bad about leaving you in the lurch, too, Griff."

I just shrug. Whatever. My head is too full of stuff to think about Guy Martin right now. The whole day is a blur of weird half-impressions, most of them circling around a dark bus and the sound of Brad crying. And the sight of Guy passed out on the Courvilles' couch. And Rosie and me in the mudroom.

I'd just like to blot it all out. Well, okay, maybe not the Rosie part.

"I need sleep." I drag myself to my feet. "Night, guys."

"What a day you've had." Mom stands up and hugs me before I stagger off to bed. "Don't set your alarm, buddy. You need sleep. I'll call the school."

I can hear them still talking downstairs when I turn off my light.

My phone buzzes and, of course, it's Blair again.

She's been calling and texting all night—a huge backlog of messages and texts that I tried to quickly reply to when Dad left to take the Courvilles home, sometime just before midnight.

What's happening? Why aren't you answering? Are you okay? Heard your interview on the late news. My famous boyfriend!!! Evan says you sounded stoned. HAHA!

I've avoided her as long as I can, I guess.

I'm ok. Tired. Check in tomorrow?

More texts, more questions. The truth is, I don't know quite what to say to her right now. So, the last thing I do on this crazy day is turn off my phone and sleep.

PHONE,
PART TWO

"Hey, Griffin. Josh Drouin here."

Of course I know it's Josh, since his name flashes up on my screen, but I play it cool. Well, as cool as you can, when you just woke up a few minutes ago, and you're still lying in bed. And it's noon.

"Hi, Josh." I sit up, because people can tell when you're talking on a phone lying down.

"Listen, I just wanted to thank you again for that interview yesterday. Sorry if it was kind of bad timing, but that's the life of a news event, eh? Get it fast, get out of there."

"No, no problem. It was fine. I didn't mind doing it at all."

"How are you feeling today? Okay? No injuries?"

I'm upright now, leaning back against the headboard. Shoulder's a bit tight, but not the usual pain. One hip might be feeling it a bit, too, but clearly my bouncing around the bus yesterday hasn't left any real issues. I'm lucky, because the word from Murph last night was that Brad won't be back on the ice for a while.

I'll have to call him, I think. Go visit. I know what it's like ...

"I'm fine. Looks like no one had any big injuries, just some bumps and bruises. Except for Brad Scott, of course."

"Yeah, you guys are lucky. I'm glad it ended up okay. In fact, the OPP reported no fatalities, so a happy ending to a scary event."

"That's great." My stomach rumbles because, of course, it's noon and I'm now awake and starving. I can smell bacon. *Oh, Mom, you're awesome ...*

"Listen, Griff, I'll let you go," Josh says. The guy has impeccable timing. "But I just wanted to let you know that you've got some talent for media, clearly, and if you ever have questions, I'm happy to point you toward some good contacts. You know, J-school programs, internships, that kind of thing."

"Wow. Thanks. Thanks a lot." I hope I don't sound as stunned as I feel right now. "That's really nice of you. I appreciate it."

"No problem. I got a lot of help when I started out." He laughs then. "Including my time at The Legend 99.1. I got quite the education there."

"Yeah," I say. "Me, too." Of course, I don't elaborate on last night's adventures, but something tells me he may know something about Guy Martin and adventures.

"Take care, Griff."

"Thanks again, Josh. Bye."

I sit there for a moment, staring at the light around my window, and picturing myself in a media scrum at the Canadian Tire Centre. Only this time, I'm the one with the mic; I'm the one asking the questions; I'm the one with the camera guy trailing down the hall behind me.

Oh, yeah, I can see it.

I can also smell that bacon, but just as I'm beginning to think about maybe getting out of bed, my phone rings again and I see Guy's name.

"Hi, Griff. How are you doing today?"

He sounds—I don't know—he sounds perfectly normal. Everyday voice, no note of apology. Clearly not embarrassed. Or hungover. Okay.

"I'm good, thanks."

"No injuries? Arm okay? Kind of a scary incident, eh?"

"No injuries. And yeah, my arm's fine." What does he want?

"Sorry I missed the trip. Well, maybe not sorry," he laughs because, of course, he's not sorry for missing the fun of being thrown around a bus in the middle of a whiteout. "Truth is, I had a job interview yesterday afternoon, but I had to keep it quiet. All out in the open now, though. I just told Elise I'll be leaving at the end of the month to move to an online media outlet out of Ottawa. Covering the Sens, mostly."

"Congratulations. That sounds great."

I keep expecting him to say something about last night, Rosie's house, my dad showing up. Maybe he doesn't remember? It's all so weird.

"So, a few more weeks of working together at The Legend, and then you're on your own," he says.

I don't know what he expects me to say, but I surprise myself—and probably him.

"You know, I'm probably going to be cutting down my hours at The Legend soon, too."

A pause. Then, "Really? Why do you say that?"

There are so many ways I could answer this question. So many images of the past few weeks flash through my mind— ending with him passed out on Rosie's couch—but I keep it simple. And maybe lie a little.

"Well, the school encourages us to try different things for our community service," I say. He doesn't know I'm skating here, but it's okay, because it's all taking shape in my head as I talk, making sense.

"Oh, they do?"

"Oh, yes. And I have this idea I've been thinking about pitching to Mr. Dunbar," I say. "Helping out at Glenavon Public School."

I'm making this up, but as I talk, it's becoming more real. And right there in the middle is the image of Noah on my driveway, trying to dangle, turning to me with that huge smile when he lifts it into the top corner. *Did you see that, Griffin?*

But I don't tell Guy. He doesn't need to know anything more about me and Noah and hockey.

"Oh, really." Guy sounds like he's not convinced, but I don't care. "I thought you had Press Box written all over you. Thought we were a pretty good team, actually."

So many things I could say here, but I don't.

"Maybe one day." No need to mention my conversation with Josh Drouin. "Lots of time to decide."

"Yes, there is. And if you want any help in that department— you know, with contacts or references or anything, like I said— just ask. Happy to help out."

"Thanks." Time to go. I'm starving and, really, we don't have anything more to say.

But he's not done.

"Oh, and Griff, listen, about last night ..."

"Forget it," I say quickly, because I really don't want to hear it.

A pause, then: "Thanks. See you at the Hawks game next week?"

"Sure, great. See you."

About last night. Maybe I should have let him explain.

No. It's time to move on.

To bacon.

RUDE BOYS

"What did he say?"

As arranged, Jake's waiting for me at the coffee shop after my trip to Dr. Fitzpatrick's office, and he already has two huge cookies and a couple of large drinks on the table in front of him.

"All clear. I can play." We high-five loudly and some older ladies at the next table glance our way. *Rude boys!* I don't care.

It's Friday afternoon, a week after my bus adventure, and Mom has just dropped me off for some guy time while she pops over to the mall.

"One hour, Griffin. Then the bus is leaving," she says as she pulls into the parking lot. "Oh, sorry. Not the best choice of words there."

But we both laugh, because the bus accident is so behind me now.

"Great news," Jake says.

"And I might even have a team."

"What?"

It's true. Coach Bedard stopped me in the corridor outside the dressing room after the Hawks game this week.

"I hear you might be looking for a team," he said. "Arm's pretty close to being healed?"

I stood there, stunned. How could he know that?

"Um ... possibly. Yeah, but ..."

Somebody coming up from behind shoves me off balance and I stumble, but Coach just grins at Brad, arm in a sling, standing there.

"Hey, Turdiff. You're looking for a team, right? As soon as the doctor gives you the green light?"

"Well ... yeah ... maybe."

"We have an opening," says Coach Bedard. "If you're interested in a tryout."

I tell Jake this, still shaking my head a little that Brad Scott, who is generally a bit of a dick, would do something like that, speak up for me. People will surprise you, my wizard mother always says and, once again, she is right.

"Have you told Blair?" Jake asks.

I take a sip and, of course, he notices the long pause. Raises one eyebrow.

"Uh ... no."

I haven't told him that Blair and I broke up. Actually, Blair doesn't know we broke up, either. I haven't told her yet, but I will. In person, because there are some things you just have to do in person. A text would be so much easier, of course, and I bet she's getting suspicious, because I haven't answered any of her calls, and my replies to her texts have been a bit limited, except for the one asking if she's going to be home this afternoon. So, Mom's going to drop me off at Blair's house on the way to supper at Bella's.

Mom sounded quite happy about it, actually. "Take as long as you need," she said, when I told her about it earlier this afternoon, as we left Glenavon and hit the highway to Ottawa. "You can walk to Bella's from there, or I can swing by and retrieve you." She has a big smile and doesn't glance at me, which tells me everything I need to know.

Now I see Jake with a look on his face that tells me he's trying to decide whether to say something, which, of course, he does.

"Evan."

I shrug. "I know."

"I wanted to tell you, but it felt too much like the playground in elementary school." He sounds relieved. "When did you figure it out?"

"I guess the weekend of the tournament. When she sent that picture from the party." I shrug. "There were other signs. I just wasn't paying attention."

Jake nods. "Sucks."

But I'm smiling because, in fact, I don't think it sucks at all.

"No, it's okay. We were doomed from the start." He grins at me.

"Too short."

We say it in unison and collapse, laughing. The ladies next door give us another look, but we rude boys just ignore them and keep laughing.

SMILE

Saturday afternoon. The sun is out, strong, and the ice is melting on the edges of the driveway, where I'm out taking shots with Noah. Almost December, but it's spring-like, sunny and almost mild.

Dangle, drag, shoot—the tidy *pffft* as the ball hits the back of the net.

The sun is warm on my back. Our jackets are tossed on the brick retaining wall on the side of the driveway. I'm wearing my team sweater from last year, and Noah is in a Junior Moose jersey, maybe borrowed from his friend Lucas.

A while ago, Mom came out and took a picture with her phone. "Hey, hockey boys!" she calls to us, and we shoulder up to each other and smile. "Perfect."

Back to business. He actually manages a drag and lifts the ball into the net.

"Did you see that?" he grins, retrieving the ball, ready to do it again.

"Great shot. Hey, Noah? Would you like to play hockey? For real, I mean? Skates and equipment and everything?"

He stickhandles in place for a few swipes, thinking.

"No. Maybe one day. I just like doing this."

He takes another shot and raises his arms, as if he just scored the winning goal.

"Yeah, me, too, Noah. This is good."

This past week, Mike and I talked to Mr. Dunbar about a possible community service project for the spring: an after-school ball hockey league for the kids at the elementary school. Noah's school. We have a meeting with the principal next week to talk about it. And Elise Rogers has no problem reducing my hours at The Legend and letting me juggle both. She tells me I'll probably win the community service prize for my grade. Whatever.

"What do you think of this idea, Noah? Would you and some of your friends like to play ball hockey at school? You know, in the gym, maybe? I'm thinking about suggesting it to your school, with a friend of mine. What do you think?"

He's intent on practicing his dangle and doesn't look up. Tongue between his teeth.

"That would be cool." And then he stops and looks at me. "You'd be there, right?"

"Yeah, I'd be there."

"And we could still come here, just you and me, and play here sometimes, too?"

"Of course. Whenever you want."

"Then, yeah, that would be good."

He takes another shot, and then he asks if we can play our special passing game, the one we invented that requires intense concentration and much yelling back and forth, so I don't notice her until she's at the end of the driveway. Noah does, though.

"Rosie! Watch!" He executes three perfect passes and buries the ball in the net. Arms in the air. "Winning goal!"

"Way to go," she calls to him. "First star, Noah."

She's wearing that long green sweater again, over her black jeans and boots. And a striped knitted scarf around her neck, fingerless mittens on her hands. Her sketch pad is tucked under her arm. No hat, and the sun reflects off her dark hair. I want to tell her she's beautiful.

She doesn't say anything to me, though. Doesn't even look at me. She just finds a spot on the brick wall near our discarded jackets and settles her sketch pad on her lap. I watch her hand, the one holding the pencil, as it swoops over the page a few times, like a bird over water. She looks at her brother, thinking, watching. Then she drops her eyes to the blank page and starts to draw.

"Rosie, guess what? Griffin's going to talk to my school

about us kids playing ball hockey. In the gym. Sort of like us on the driveway, but with other kids."

"That's nice," she says, drawing him in action. Drawing both of us, maybe.

See me, Rosie. I see you. Look up.

Noah's already turned away, stickhandling up the driveway.

Rosie. Look up.

She doesn't look up, but it doesn't matter. She knows I'm standing there watching her, and she's smiling.

ACKNOWLEDGMENTS

Writing fiction is fun because I get to make things up, but in writing The Legend, I knew I would need some real-life details. I had help along the way, and if readers find it hard to suspend their disbelief, please forgive me for taking liberties in order to serve the purposes of my story.

Thanks, Georgia Atkinson, friend and retired ER nurse, for your clinical details concerning a broken humerus bone in a young athlete, and what he would experience during his recovery.

Two former colleagues on the Media and Communications team at Curling Canada had a big impact on how I portrayed Griffin's media experiences. Al Cameron, my former boss, taught me how to write a coherent game summary; how to herd reporters into an orderly post-game scrum; and how to laugh through long hours in a cold arena, amid the chaos of a national championship. And Danielle Inglis, media pro and elite athlete, showed me what a powerful storytelling tool social media can be when it's done well.

Hockey Night in Canada broadcaster Chris Cuthbert, my former colleague at CFRC Queen's Radio, gave me a virtual tour of the press box at the Canadian Tire Centre in Ottawa, and provided me with details to make Griffin's experience there come alive. I'm so grateful for your help, Chris, and for your support of my writing.

Thanks to the collegial Canadian kidlit community for social media boosts and conversations. Special thanks to two writerly friends, Heather Wright and Lorna Schultz Nicholson, for your unfailing support—and for your pep talks!

Thank you, Peter Carver, my editor at Red Deer Press, for believing in my writing and making my dream of being a published author a reality—three times! Thanks also to copy editor Penny Hozy for making me look good on paper.

I'm grateful to the Ontario Arts Council, who provided financial support during the early stages of writing this novel.

Finally, thank you, Barb Bangay, for socially distanced porch teas, during which we put the world to rights. And to my home team—I couldn't do this without you.

INTERVIEW WITH JEAN MILLS

What led you to want to tell this story?

Years ago, I was driving through a small Ontario town, listening to the local radio station. The announcer was awful—affected voice, completely annoying. I thought to myself, "Imagine working with someone like that ..." And then, because my imagination always defaults to stories about teenagers, I envisioned some poor high school student dealing with a boss who doesn't inspire confidence or admiration. That moment simmered for years, and it finally became the story of Griffin and his flawed broadcasting mentor, Guy Martin.

In this "bad boss at the radio station" idea, I wanted a teen who steps up and makes things better. I found inspiration in a moment shared widely on social media, between Montreal goalie Carey Price and a grieving little boy who was invited to meet him after practice. Price, still in his gear, sees how overwhelmed

the boy is, drops his stick and gloves, and wraps him in a hug. It's a lovely moment that stuck with me and inspired the special relationship between Griffin and Noah, an important thread in *The Legend*.

You have had experience in the professional sports world for some time. To what extent did this experience affect your portrayal of the people who work for the radio station called The Legend?

I had so much fun using details from my experience on the Media and Communications team for Curling Canada to fill out Griffin's budding sports reporter experience in The Legend.

My job was simple: watch games, interview athletes, write game summaries, and keep the social media stories rolling. The media bench was teeming with reporters and broadcasters. We shared early mornings, late nights, deadlines, and bad arena food. I tried to bring some of that frenzy into Griffin's experience as a reporting intern.

As for the media people portrayed in the story, all I can say is that sports reporting seems to attract some of the nicest, oddest, and most hard-working professionals I've ever met. Yes, there were a few Guy Martins, but there were even more Josh Drouins and Elise Rogers, generous and helpful.

There are no villains in *The Legend*, but most would agree with Griffin that Guy is "a jerk." In fact, he drives a lot of the action in the story. What led you to developing Guy as an important character here?

I love writing characters like Griffin, who step up to fix things when someone is acting badly. The "jerk" could have been one of his peers, of course, but I felt there was something even more compelling about Griffin having to deal with a questionable adult, someone who isn't dangerous, but whose flaws are deep and far-reaching. Guy's lack of responsibility affects Griffin's job at The Legend. It's also Guy's inability to deal with his own demons that drives Griffin's growing interest in Rosie and Noah.

So, yes, there are no villains here, but certainly "a jerk" who is a catalyst for much of the action in this story.

Once Griffin meets Noah, he begins to think about how much it costs for kids who are getting involved with organized hockey. What are the chances these days for kids interested in hockey to find ways of playing pick-up games, rather than getting involved in organized leagues?

One of the cherished memories of my childhood is of falling asleep to the sound of pucks echoing off the boards at the outdoor rink down the street—my big brothers playing hockey with their friends. These days, ice time is scarce at community arenas, so the days of kids congregating at the local rink for some shinny are long gone. Some parks create rinks during the winter, but I've seen "No Hockey" signs posted, too, probably for safety reasons.

Hockey is an expensive sport, too expensive for many families. Programs do exist to make the sport more affordable, so maybe there's hope that a more recreational, inclusive approach to hockey is coming back.

Griffin and Rosie are brought together because they live close to each other, and also because Noah finds Griffin a new and important person in his young life. Yet, at school, some of Griffin's classmates want to make more of the Rosie/Griffin connection by creating gossip about them. To what extent do you think this is typical of the high school scene?

High school is such a perfect place for drama—all the "types" are there, and young people are constantly trying to figure out where they fit in. So, when a new character arrives on the scene—in this case, Griffin, a smart, cool guy adopted by the jocks—it's natural that he'd be on display. And a girl like Rosie, who tends to keep herself apart, is an unusual focus for such a boy. I think in any high school, especially in a small community, any interaction between Griffin and Rosie would result in lots of attention and gossip.

From the outset, Griffin isn't certain how settled he and Blair are in their relationship. In fact, one might wonder whether it would even work if Griffin didn't have to move away for a year. What do you think is missing in their relationship that makes it so uncertain?

I think their relationship is unequal, and probably based on physical attraction and their status as school athletes, more than any deep connection. Blair is confident and assured, a talented athlete and very attractive (as Griffin mentions more than once). But she's also cold. She doesn't seem to understand Griffin's emotional needs—missing hockey, exiled from his Ottawa friends. She wants him there, but he's more of a cool appendage than an equal partner. And Griffin senses this: he refers to her as "Blair, my is-she-or-isn't-she girlfriend," which suggests he knows she's not all in and maybe can't be trusted.

But Griffin has a strong sense of self. He doesn't need his relationship with Blair to make him feel complete. That's why Rosie and her vulnerability, and her appreciation for his kindness toward Noah, gets through to him. What he feels for Rosie is a true emotional connection: "Holding Blair never felt like this."

What do you think the prospects are for the Griffin/ Rosie relationship?

Oh, I think the prospects are very good. But I think they still have a lot to learn about each other. He's seen her in fierce big sister mode, in school mode, but he's also seen her connecting warmly with the seniors at the Avonlea. She's seen him at school but also happily playing ball hockey with her little brother, and he's there when she needs him. He'll only be around until the end of the school year, but I see these two independent young people finding a way to build a relationship that might last, based on what they've learned about each other so far.

In the three novels you have done with Red Deer, you explore the fascinating world of teen-agers' social and emotional concerns. What has provided you with the insights into that world when, as an adult, you are years from experiencing it at first hand?

I remember my emotionally high-low teenage years as if they happened yesterday. I also wrote a lot of terrible poetry and kept diaries, which I still have, if I ever need to dive back into that time.

But I'm also a mother. My kids are both past their teenage years now, but their experiences are deeply imprinted on me. My daughter and son are very different people (both wonderful human beings, I'm happy to say), and their teenage years were completely different experiences. I saw and learned a lot.

On top of this, I was a community college professor for fifteen years, and many of my students were fresh out of high school. I can't begin to describe the cross-section of styles, attitudes, behaviors and maturity, not to mention the highs and lows of their lives, that I witnessed or even played a role in during those years.

The landscape changes, of course—world events, technology, social media, for example—but I believe the teenage experience will always be an emotional, unpredictable journey toward adulthood, and I love writing about kids on that journey.

An important character from a previous novel of yours, Nathan McCormick, appears briefly in this story. Might he reappear as a central figure in a future Jean Mills novel?
I would love to write about Nathan again! It was fun to bring him back briefly in *The Legend*, but there's lots more to explore in his story—especially how his unsettled early life made him the strong, principled person he is in *Skating Over Thin Ice*, and what's next for him (and Imogen) as he deals with the pressures of an NHL career. I confess, I've been thinking about this, too ...

Thank you, Jean, for all your thoughtful insights.